Peter and the Electric Overlords

By
P F Haskins

Copyright © 2021 P F Haskins

All Rights Reserved

ISBN-13: 9798735669593

Peter and the Electric Overlords

Chapter 1

The three of them ate in silence. Peter looked at his father, forcefully stabbing his fork into the spring potatoes, head bowed and intent only on the contents of his plate. Then he glanced over to his mother and caught the movement of her eyes as they flickered from plate upwards, as if checking if anything novel had happened, or was likely to. Even with the radio playing, the absence of sound was heavy and sad. But even if he could, Peter knew better than to break it. It was an adult's silence, and he was an eight year old boy.

Besides, today, the habitual silence of the family's mealtime seemed appropriate. More in keeping with the mood of the world. Peter had felt it rising over recent days, at home, and especially at school, where teachers had huddled together in urgent whispers, and their hollow eyes had betrayed an unaccustomed uncertainty. Today's unusual afternoon assembly had been a conclusion of sorts. Yet Mr Chamber's sombre announcement that none of them would be returning to school the following Monday had still been a surprise. It carried none of the head teacher's usual confidence. Even the younger pupils of St George's Primary School, Arneby, sitting cross legged and keen, had fidgeted less, struck dumb by the unease which Mr Chambers had been unable to mask. It was like they were turning off school for a long time, pulling over the dust sheets. It was the falling pitch of a spent machine.

Peter couldn't remember a time when they didn't listen to the news bulletin during dinner. And it was only after he had gone for a sleepover at James Ancaster's house that the contrast with his own family had come into relief. Over dinner, Mr Ancaster had been eager to question both boys about their life at school, and Peter had tingled as the conversation bounced between members of the Ancaster clan. He couldn't say if the solemnity of their own meals was better or worse than that of the Ancasters', only different.

Yet now, the events of the day demanded a keen quiet, and Peter felt the novelty of paying attention to the words of the radio for the first time. They came in spurts.

'Quite possibly comes from bats...zoonosis disease...corona virus...support package for rough sleepers...no need to panic buy...until further notice...covid 19...postpone non-urgent operations...key workers...panic buying...the end of the world as we know it...from China...covid crisis...avoid pubs and restaurants...non-essential travel...self-isolate...rise in new cases...pre existing medical conditions...covid'

'What will you do?' The question was barely audible over the stream from the radio, and Peter wondered if his mother had regretted it. She had already returned her gaze to the table. A different quality of quiet fell between them, and Peter could hear his father chewing over the question.

'About what?' his father finally said. He didn't look up, and Peter recognised the moroseness in his voice, unwilling to take the conversation further. Here it would normally end, but today was not normal, and Peter winced at the insistence he heard in his mother's reply.

'About your work,' she hissed. 'Are you going to close?'

'I don't know, yet.'

'What about the staff?'

'I said, I don't know, yet.'

'But you said you're already seeing orders drying up. How will you keep the staff on if you've got no work? The Government are saying all businesses have to close.'

'Donna, I'll work it out, alright. There's only five of them to sort out anyway. And they say the Government's going to come up with a scheme to help companies.'

'But that's not going to pay all their wages, is it?'

Peter looked at his mother. Her eyes were puffy and red, and the darker streaks in her blond hair were unordered. They gave her a wild, needy look. Peter wasn't sure if he admired or pitied her stubborn insistence.

'It might do,' his father replied.

'That's not what Mrs Proudfoot reckons.'

'I don't care what Mrs Proudfoot thinks. She's not running my company.'

'But she says the Government isn't likely to pay all their wages, and that employers will have to foot the bill for the difference.'

'Since when did Mrs Proudfoot become an expert on Government policy? They don't even know themselves what they're doing. They're just making it up the spot. Like the rest of us.' He paused, satisfied, it seemed, by the conclusion he had arrived at. He finished with a flourish. 'You shouldn't listen to her so much anyway. She's full of crap.'

Peter felt the weight of his mother's shifted gaze, checking if the harsh word had affected him. His father, despite his better education, was oblivious to such things.

'That's not fair, Steve.'

'Isn't it? You've been spending too much time with her.'

'She's just someone to talk to.'

'She's a busybody, that's what she is. I don't know what you see in her.'

'She's the only one around here who's even half friendly.'

'What about all the mums at school? They're more your age.'

Peter saw the hint of a smirk emerge at the creased corner of his father's lip, but it was a cruel blow. In the six months they had spent in the new village, in the new house, Peter's mother had remained resolutely alone at the school gates at three-thirty, distanced from the gaggle of mothers chatting without reserve closer to the door from which the pupils would daily emerge. Peter didn't know if his mother had made any attempt to penetrate the mums' group, but if she had, it had been unsuccessful.

A cry from the end of the heavy pine table forestalled any response, and Peter watched as his mother pushed back the matching wooden chair, not bothering to lift it and letting it scrape the floor, before padding the few steps to the cot in which his baby sister had briefly roused herself. He watched as his mother leant over, close to the wrappings of the child, whispering, hushing, soothing. Even from the other side of the table, Peter could feel the weight of attention the child was receiving. It was a love with a double edge, for ever since the child's birth he had felt his mother's interest slip away from him, towards the new arrival.

It wasn't that she loved him less. He could still slip into her bed and receive a sleepy cuddle, or be wrapped in embrace at the end of a school day. The warmth in her eyes when she looked at him was still keen. Rather, he knew he was just less in her thoughts. Less present than he had once been. The arrival of the new child had knocked him from the close orbit around her, away from the warm mother star, outward, to beyond the cold, rocky asteroids.

When she returned to the table, they continued the meal without speaking. The voices on the radio had moved on to the following day's weather, but none of the three was paying attention. The conversation wasn't finished, and all three knew it. Peter felt his father poised, like a tree bound predator, a dark panther in the shadows, waiting for the opportunity to leap down. Peter felt, as much as heard, the intake of breath as his mother steadied herself to speak once more.

'I'm just worried about the mortgage, Steve, that's all.'

His father lanced a final potato, using it to scrape up the remains of the sauce around his plate, but remained silent.

'How are we supposed to pay the mortgage if the company shuts down and you've got no work?' his mother continued.

Peter had heard the word before. Mortgage. It had been a regular guest in their house, ever since their move from the centre of Halfdenport to the new village and semi-private street with high hedges and manicured properties. Mortgage. His father had used the word with pride, talking about its size with the same unction he reserved for his other favourites; his sleek, brooding car, the company's turnover, the size of the garden in the new house, and, when the mood took him, his wife's beauty.

But now there was no pride, only a quiet anger as his father continued to stare at the empty plate. It was an anger that always first appeared through the eyes, tightening into hard, dark knots which gradually lit up from within, like someone stoking a fire in a night forge.

'We'll manage,' he finally said, though without conviction.

'How? We're paying nearly half your earnings into the mortgage, and every month we struggle to make ends meet. We've got nothing to fall back on if we can't meet those payments!'

'I said, we'll manage.' And for the first time, Peter's father looked up, directly at his wife, challenging her. Peter saw the tendons in his father's fingers as they gripped the edge of the table. Briefly, his mother offered her defiance by meeting her husband's eyes, and Peter could feel their wills locking across the family dining table. It wasn't fear he felt at such moments, only sadness. A wearying sadness. He longed to be away.

His father might have heard his thoughts. Sometimes he could do that, an ability which unsettled Peter.

'Peter, have you finished?' he said, looking over at the boy. Peter nodded.

'Then go to your room. I want to talk to Mummy about something.'

'Don't you want any pudding, darling?' his mother offered.

'He can have it later,' said his father, putting an end to the conversation. Peter needed no second invitation and hopped down from the chair which was still too big for him, and scooted through the hall, picking up the electronic square from the table where he had left it, then scurrying on all fours, monkey like, up the carpeted stairs, into his bedroom, closing the door firmly before leaping onto the bed. He waited a moment, letting his ears clear themselves of the rush upstairs, then listening carefully to see if his parents' argument was likely to follow him. But all was quiet, and Peter felt the calmness that always came with entry into his own world.

Yet the peace dragged something else, something heavy and dark, something that couldn't be ignored or shut away. The end of school, the grim daily news, his parents' frustrations and arguments. Why was all of this happening? A danger was creeping around the edges of their lives. But what was it? What had so disturbed the core of the everyday? Was it war? An invasion from a foreign power? From another world? Were their lives at risk? Was this what the threat of real death felt like?

Peter was sure of one thing. It did feel very real. As real as that first week at the new school when, still without friends, fat gypsy boy Sean McCracken had stabbed him with a biro for no reason, then stood by to watch his reaction, before his friendship with local farmer's son James Ancaster had made his presence at the new school safer and more bearable.

This new danger felt like an enemy. Something which needed to be taken on and defeated. Just as he had already done with the hordes who never ceased attacking their house via the back garden. No matter how close they came, even as they spilled over the slight rise between back lawn and arable field, Peter would still fend them off, often resorting to vicious hand to hand fighting in the last desperate metres before they reached his den, his HQ. The new menace would be dispatched in a similar way.

Yet Peter knew a good general must rely on cunning and intelligence as much as sheer strength of numbers and weaponry, and whatever it was that was troubling Mr Chambers, agitating the wise people behind the daily news, and playing havoc between his parents, it demanded different weapons to the rifles, arrows and swords with which he drove his enemies away from the back garden. This enemy was faceless and vague, everywhere and nowhere.

Peter put his hand down onto the duvet, and with one adept movement picked up and turned on the Eye Pad, transforming the grey reflective screen into a blaze of colours; the mist covered tree tops against the russet lines of a fading sun and sky. Peter had never seen such trees before, but that was the whole point of the Eye Pad, taking the mind's eye to places and times that outdid even the strongest imagination. Details were unimportant, it was the images that mattered, his launch pad to another world, another adventure. From climbing the great pyramids of Egypt to being dragged by dogs across the harsh Arctic tundra, from marching with his legion through a triumphal arch on his Roman homecoming to loosening a whole quiver of arrows against the Dauphin's knights at Agincourt, all this, and more, he had done with his jabbing, swishing index figure.

But now was no moment for a frivolous adventure. Now, he had a mission. The enemy had a name. Covid. He had heard it barely twenty minutes previously. They had never tired of repeating it. Covid. It had the power of mantra. Covid. Know thy enemy. Covid.

Peter summoned the keyboard on the Eye Pad. He felt clumsy with the letters, awkward lines and loops that reminded him that, however much he wanted to enjoy reading, spelling was still an ordeal for him. He much preferred the pictures. They spoke to him in a language he was quick to understand.

Covid. He could hear the word still as his finger hovered artlessly over the black letters. The 'C' was easy, but scanning the keyboard for the 'O', he felt a familiar sense of frustration as every letter seemed to clamour for his attention. Finally, he found it, pushing down firmly, triumphantly with his finger. But what came next? Any rules behind spelling were still mysterious, and one letter was often as good as another. While others in the class just seemed to 'get' it, earning a long row of ticks in their narrow spelling test books, his tests were an ugly melange of harsh crosses with just an occasional tick, the result of luck or some deep residual memory. Knowing which letter to pick was as troublesome as deciding what means his enemies might use for attacking his den castle at the back of the house. Multiple. Unknowable.

Peter shifted his gaze along the top row of the keyboard. The 'T' looked attractive, very attractive, yet even before he had pushed the button on the screen, he had mentally added it into what he already had. C-O-T. No, the sound was wrong. Definitely wrong. But what about the neighbouring 'R', that was more promising. C-O-R. Yes, that might work. It was worth a try. He pressed the letter. C-O-R. Yes, that definitely looked possible, maybe even probable. Fortune favours the brave. He would go with it.

The 'V' was easier. He rehearsed again the word from the radio and, yes, the 'V' was the very essence of the word, the heart of the enemy. Now, halfway there, the rest was easy, and Peter began to wonder why he had doubted himself. The 'I' and the 'D' were simple, like riding his bike downhill, they required little effort, and he experienced a brief sense of satisfaction as he looked at the completed word on the screen, C-O-R-V-I-D. It was an initial skirmish won. He looked at the word again, steadying himself for what the return button would bring, what images he would be faced with. A certain stoutness was required. Strength of spirit. He pressed.

He was surprised with what leapt into view from the image search. Apart from the variation in background, each photo was practically the same. Birds. Black, ragged birds, whose tatty feathers reminded him of the collages they liked so much at school, pieces glued and heaped on to the other. So, this was it. He hadn't expected that.

With his curiosity aroused, he scrolled down the screen, letting his finger scrape lazily down the pane of glass, watching as subtle varieties of the thing came into view, some as black as coal, others a lighter grey, some with a sheen which exposed the fault lines of their feathers, others a flattening, deadening matt. But as his eyes followed each phalanx of squares from left to right, then back again, one thing began to stand out from all else; the beak of the creatures. Thick and solid as it emerged from their fragile heads, its slight curve hinting of grace and beauty, yet ending in a point that looked as sharp and deadly as any sword which Peter had ever pitted himself against. Here was a weapon of substance. Infinitely malleable, the initial thrust would break the skin, a second entrance would see the pointers open, clasping with iron vigour whatever soft tissue they had touched upon, then viciously wrenching it all from the body of the host. It would be carnage.

Peter didn't need to see any more. Now he understood why Mr Chambers hadn't wished to give details of the school closure, or why the teachers had looked so pitifully at the young children – it was their unblemished skin which would be split open under the beaks of such creatures, like tearing tissue paper. Covid, Peter realised, was worse than he had imagined.

The creatures' eyes spoke of a deeper malice. What they lacked in size, they made up for in spirit, each one intensely fixed upon some unseen object. Peter always knew the Eye Pad was an interface, a window onto another world which he could open or close as the mood took him. But this was different. Now the eyes of the Covids, beady and keen, were really looking at him. Somehow they had tricked their way through the defences of the Eye Pad, broken through the screen. The deadly Covid, here, in the sanctuary of his own bedroom. A chill ran through him and he wondered if he should turn the machine off before they got any further. Little wonder that the whole world was quaking, and Peter didn't need to read the snippets of descriptions below each image which talked of the intelligence and cleverness of these creatures, he could already feel it. He suddenly felt very alone in his silent room. It would be a campaign like no other. These Covids would be a formidable enemy.

Chapter 2

Setting the Eye Pad back on the duvet, Peter sat still, thinking. Below, he could hear the sound of plates and cutlery being cleared away, a door closing. His parents, it seemed, had finished and his presence would no longer be resented. Besides, the revelation of the Covids had been a shock, filling him with a strong need to share. To show them that he, too, understood what the panic was about, that he was ready and willing to play a part in ridding the world of the threat.

He padded quietly down the stairs, moving silently across the hall. To his right, he could hear the television in the living room, ahead of him, the glass door to the kitchen, through which he could see his mother hunched over the sink, her head bowed, resolutely scrubbing. Peter watched her for a moment. She must have felt something, because she turned, fixing him immediately and offering a weak smile. Instinctively, Peter responded, hoping his own grimace would do something to lift her. But he didn't enter. He had no wish to be with his mother like this, not when anything he said would slide off her despondency. Being with his father was less complicated.

'Hello, Son,' his father said as Peter pushed open the door to the living room.

'Hi, Dad.' Peter looked at his father, sprawled at an angle across the sofa. He could see where the flesh at his waist line stretched the fabric of the work shirt, a mid-thirties battle which his father had given up on winning, much like the harsh crew cut which did away with the grey which had recently begun to menace the ends of the voluminous brown hair, the same bouncy waves which had so attracted his mother at the beginning of their courtship.

His father stretched an arm out, drawing Peter towards him, onto the comfortable sofa, and Peter smelt a familiar odour, male adult mixed with the sharp chemicals of the printing presses of his work. It was uniquely his father, and it made Peter happy. His father could be indulgent when it pleased him and, while Peter was now old enough to be wary of such switches in mood, he never tired of falling under its spell. It was as though his father was keen to make amends for his harshness at the dinner table.

'Fancy watching the film with me?'

Peter smiled in response and felt the extra pressure on his shoulder as his father pulled him closer.

The film was a noisy affair, filled with explosions, collapsing buildings and desperate dialogue. It was like nothing Peter experienced in his everyday life in Arneby, but the boundaries of where one reality began and the other finished were still blurry. Maybe there really were places where this kind of thing happened. Maybe he was just living in the wrong town.

Peter soon realised his father had seen the film before. It was the kind of film his father liked. A creature from another planet had been found, though its intentions were not kind. The flashing, swiftly changing images transfixed Peter, but he found it difficult to follow the storyline.

'Dad, why are the aliens trying to kill the humans?'

'I don't know, Son. Perhaps they just don't like them.'

'Why?'

'Because they're different to them,' said his father. Peter was unsure if it was a question or an answer.

'Oh.'

'Or maybe because they want to take over the earth, and the humans are in the way.'

'Oh.'

Peter was quiet for a moment. His father's eyes hadn't moved from the screen, where one of the main characters was speaking to the crew of a ship, all young and shiny with sweat and studio make up. Everyone was attentive and serious. '*We're not going down without a fight*,' he pronounced, while the others looked on approvingly. The world now depended on them.

'Dad?'

'Mmmm.'

'Are the Covids like the aliens?'

'The Covids?'

On the screen an alien craft had emerged, dripping and masterful, from the sea. The music score swelled. Peter could see the reflection of the alien ship in his father's stunned eyes.

'Yes, the Covids, the thing everyone's getting so worried about.'

'That's just a virus, Son. I wouldn't get worried about it. It'll be over in a few weeks.' His father sat up. 'Watch this bit, Son. Watch what the alien craft does.'

Peter turned to watch, but he was growing weary of the film. It seemed very distant. He knew that his world would remain unchanged when the final credits rolled. It always did. And the aliens weren't the real threat. It was the Covids, the beasts he had seen earlier. Mr Chambers, the other teachers, the people on TV, they all knew how serious the situation was. Maybe his father was just being brave for him, using the film as a distraction.

Peter slipped below his father's limp arm. He made no effort to stop Peter and didn't look away from the screen as Peter hopped nimbly over the cushioned arm of the sofa and out of the room.

He would have returned upstairs to his own room, but the kitchen was now empty. His mother must have gone upstairs with his sister Julia. Briefly, Peter wondered if he should go to see her, but the empty kitchen presented an opportunity. There was still some light in the sky so he would be able to make out some details in his den. It would be a chance to consolidate, to ponder his next moves.

The garden was long and thin. Nothing like as large as the playing field at school, but much bigger than the box garden of their last house. Hedges ran to either side of the strip of lawn but the bottom was open, dipping slightly to the large field which stretched down to a track about half a mile away. Beyond this, the land rose again in fields, boundary hedges and the occasional house, until it met the horizon, many miles away. It was the nameless place his enemies always oozed from as they began their long assault.

He walked slowly across the grass, half wishing he had tied the laces on his trainers, past the goal post which was in the same position his father had first positioned it, facing away from the house, towards the other goal. Its immaculate white netting shone brightly in the fading light, and in the warm stillness of the evening Peter felt it as something alive, its reproach even more intense than normal.

Twenty more steps and he reached his destination; the other goal. Though in the dim light it could have been a large boulder or sleeping bear. The mouth had been turned away from the other goal, towards the open field. Over the frame, Peter had draped several blankets and old sheets found in the garage. Clothes pegs stood erect from the coverings where he had clipped them onto the netting. Whatever misgivings he had passing the first goal evaporated here, his HQ, his command centre. Two uneven coverings met at the front, like a tent, which Peter swept aside as he crouched down to crawl into the space he had created. Not for the first time, he experienced a sense of satisfaction as his knees came to land on the fabric he had carefully laid out as a carpet over the harsher grass. Letting the flaps fall back behind him, the sudden darkness was his friend. He was at home.

In the shelter of his tented keep, Peter was happy to let the strange day play with him; that he wouldn't be returning to school after the weekend, that Mr Chambers and Year 4's own Ms Parsley would soon become strangers to him, that his own mother would no longer ferry messages from James Ancaster's mother about sleepovers, and that the new house and its generous boundaries would be his limits from now on. All this until the curse of the Covids was overcome.

Time grew plastic inside the darkness, so when he heard the sharp notes of a bird ring clearly and precisely close by, he couldn't say if he had been one minute or ten ensconced inside his den, absorbing the day's unusual happenings. The sound came in volleys, half a dozen quickly struck notes followed by a satisfied trill, almost a gurgling, like a full stop, clearing the way for the next salvo.

It was too close to ignore, and Peter moved quickly, thrusting his head from the flaps, scanning quickly from left to right, the brown hair of his long fringe rising and falling with the movement. Nothing. Only the wall like shape of hedge on either side, while staring hard down to the fields below, all the details of the landscape had already dissolved into night.

It was only when Peter was still again, his head emerging from the folds of the shelter like a pantomime villain, that he caught the stabbing movement to his left, beneath the black slab of laurel. As Peter turned, the creature jumped again, a jerky, graceless set of movements, which brought it beyond the darkness of the hedge. But even in the crepuscular light, the bird's colour was unmistakeable. Black. The colour of death.

Peter's heart rose and fell like a devilish fairground ride, up and down, up then crashing down. It was a Covid, right here in front of him. Fear stalled him and he was unable to move. It had come for him. Ambushed him, in the heart of his territory, his fiefdom, his domain. It had come to add him to the piles of dead which were accumulating by the moment. The creature hadn't even given him time for words of farewell to his parents.

The Covid was barely two metres away. And it was not releasing its gaze, so close that Peter could see the remaining light gleaming off the aqueous surface of the creature's eye. An eye that was missing nothing. It was like a Western shootout, where each man waited to see who was the first to lose their nerve. But Peter's pistol was empty. He wasn't even curious about how it was going to end, it just was. Maybe it didn't even matter how. For a moment Peter wondered what people would say about him when he was gone. Would they really miss him?

Yet the creature made no bold move to come closer, content, it seemed, to examine Peter only and, as the moments passed, and he remained alive, Peter, too, began to look with interest more than fear, examining the Covid more closely, playing back the images he had seen earlier, lining them up against this example whose spindle legs were poised between the broken twigs and decaying leaves of previous years' windfall.

And he noticed the differences. This Covid seemed smaller, or if not smaller, more frail, less robust. Sleeker as well, less inclined to the ragged, careless appearance of the harsher Covids. And maybe, just maybe, not quite as black. In fact, altogether a softer creature.

And then, the bird, as if saluting the conclusion that Peter had reached, released the same startling, clear call he had heard previously. It caused him to look at the beak for the first time as it opened and closed precisely, like an elastic band pulling back into shape. And that was it. The difference. Yellow. The beak was yellow, or rather egg yolk. It was a splash of colour that confirmed that this was no Covid, whose blackness had been complete. Around the eyes, too, a fine ring of the same colour.

Peter felt his body sag and, as he did so, the bird erupted again, louder, as if it, too, was sharing Peter's relief. Now Peter smiled, throwing it out directly to the bird, who hopped further from the safety of the laurel hedge, towards Peter, its head twisting in small, digital movements, first one way, then the other, until finally coming to rest on Peter, who stared back. Like this, the bird released a final trill, almost triumphant in tone, and without doubt aimed at Peter who could only smile back, relief now swelled by happiness. And then, before the final notes had floated away into the evening air, the bird turned sharply, half scampering, half flying into the darkness beneath the wide laurel leaves.

'Goodbye, little friend,' called Peter into the growing silence.

Chapter 3

When he woke, Peter did the same as he had done every day since school had finished, almost a week ago now. He went to his parents' bedroom, across the landing where the orange nightlight was still on. The room was dark and, even peering in, Peter could see the curtains drawn across the windows which looked over the front of the house, across the shingle of the semi-circular driveway and narrow road beyond. Even at the threshold of the door, the air was stuffy and full of the night's passage. As his eyes grew accustomed to the gloom, Peter could see the outline of his mother under the covers. Little Julia would be somewhere close to her, too. And both would still be sleeping, recovering from another haphazard night.

Peter thought he might have heard them, though it could have been part of his dream. Or another night, entirely. In these unusual days, time was already starting to unwind. At the very least, this morning wouldn't be one in which he could slide in to one side of the double bed, feel the humid security of his mother and gasp and giggle with his baby sister. His father, he knew, would be long gone. He had returned to work at the start of the week, without his staff, a captain going down with his ship. Peter couldn't remember the last time he had found both parents together in bed.

Turning away, Peter stepped slowly downstairs. He could feel the stillness of the interior as he descended. The fact that the radio had been left on only added to the eerie effect. And he realised that again he would have to prepare his own breakfast, pouring out the cereal from the packet, retrieving the milk from the fridge, the silent slide of the cutlery drawer. It had been the same on Monday, three days ago. At first it had been odd, having neither parent around to layer and arrange his experience. But nothing about this period, this lockdown as it was being called, was normal. Everything carried with it an edge of the unknown.

Peter stopped at the downstairs toilet. He preferred this facility to the larger bathroom, upstairs. It was more intimate, inviting reflection somehow. This might also have something to do with the scroll which hung directly opposite the user, making it difficult to miss. Inside the frame, the paper appeared faded to the colour of ripe wheat, with darker stains to the edges hinting at the intrusion of water, though both aspects could have been deliberate design. *Desiderata*. The title ran in large ancient letters along the top of the sheet. The word was new for Peter, and he often wondered if it was even English, like the rest of the text. It had taken Peter many visits to work out that the start of each paragraph was an oversized, colourful letter, each surrounded by flowery motifs, and that the letter connected with the spidery text in the main part. Much of it Peter didn't understand. What did it mean to *feign affection,* or *take kindly the counsel of the years*? But other parts he liked, he understood, and often he would linger in front of the piece, long after nature had taken its course, moving very deliberately from word to word, enjoying the sensation of comprehension. It was like a prayer to him. *Be yourself* was a favourite. And further down, the final words, *Be cheerful*. That should have been easy advice to follow, but often it wasn't. And the last sentence. *Strive to be happy*. That didn't sound straightforward either.

When he reached the kitchen, Peter left the radio playing. It didn't seem right to turn it off. They were speaking of little else except for Covid; of the number of cases, washing hands to protect against it, admissions to hospitals, the state of lockdown restrictions and queues in shops. A sense of things falling apart, without anyone knowing how to stitch them back together.

Corona Virus. The voices on the radio used the phrase often. It was the same expression his father had used with him, but what did it mean? Peter knew what a Covid was, he had seen them, almost come face to face with one in the garden. He knew how dangerous they were. Was this *Corona Virus* the same thing? Was it cause, or effect? Result, or part of the deadly mixture? How was he to defeat the Covids if there was another layer of enemy to take on?

The rhythmic crunching of the crisp cereal in his mouth helped distract him, and the voices from the radio began to fall away. Even the stark chimes on the hour failed to rouse him, and he drifted again as a fresh reader began the news: more doom and death. Peter hardly even noticed the change as the bulletin concluded and a new voice, breezy and full of vim, took over.

'*...and that's all in an hour's time, but first Evelyn Gradd with his guests discuss the history of birds and their evolution from dinosaurs.*'

Birds. Dinosaurs. Peter let the words bed down, interested now in his own curiosity. Another voice came from the radio.

'*Hello.*' It was a man, but something caught in the speaker's throat causing him to stop. The pause was fleeting but it caught Peter's attention. It was unusual, genuine. Not the smoothness of a professional broadcaster. This was real. It was like his Dad speaking. Or Mr Chambers at assembly. The man could have been in the room with him. And the man was going to talk about birds. And Covids were birds, weren't they? Peter stopped chewing and listened.

'*Until 20 years ago, dinosaurs were widely assumed to be large lumpen lizards that became extinct millions of years ago. Discoveries in China have since show dramatically that many were fast and feathered and some survived the great extinctions and are the ancestors of our modern birds. The recently discovered Chinese fossils of feathered dinosaurs are so well preserved, scientists can even work out the feathers' colour and where they were found on the dinosaurs' bodies, and theorise about their use for displays, insulation, and in some cases perhaps, flight. Even the large tyrannosaurus, may have had downy feathers, and it appears the small velociraptors, had long quill like feathers arranged on arms that looked like wings. With me to discuss feathered dinosaurs are...*'

The conclusions to what Peter had heard arrived like heavy raindrops marking the earth. Covids were birds. Birds were the descendants of dinosaurs. Covids, therefore, had been around for many, many years. They possessed longevity. This current crisis was no flash in the pan, here today, gone tomorrow. These Covids had staying power. The enemy was, and Peter struggled with the enormity of this conclusion, far more formidable than he had first reckoned with. These beasts had been lurking in the shadows for millions of years, and only now had they decided that the time was right to strike. Peter tried to listen again. Some useful intelligence for the battles to come maybe. But the revelation about the Covids was too big. It billowed, leaving little room for more details which the speakers were beginning to address and which came in spurts...*massively successful...like dragons and monsters...great skeletons...living in slow motion...Darwin's bulldog...missing link between reptile and bird...230 million years ago... Permian extinction...Jurassic period...spread around the world...six mile wide asteroid...things change very quickly...*

He drifted away from the radio, back to himself. Who else knew all this? This endurance, this staying power through time. That Covids had once done battle with the ferocious T-Rex, laid low the brontosaurus. What chance for humans against such a force?

Each conclusion landed harder than the previous one. And, most stunning of all, the realisation that he alone, of all humans, might be the only one to have made the connection between Covids and the past. That he, Peter Lassiter, had stumbled across the heart of the matter.

But it seemed too incredible to be true. He was only eight, rarely achieved above half marks in his tests, yet in his possession he held a truth which was as clear as the window through which he now turned to look, to let it all settle. It was fine day outside, the sun would soon burn through the thin gauze of white mist which still held back the crisp blue beyond.

As he looked upwards, Peter grew aware of the radio, now just a series of disconnected, discordant sounds. Irritating. Peter quickly turned off the device, and a silence moved into the space around it. The interlude was brief.

'Peter...Peter, love.' The voice was thin and hoarse, and Peter knew his mother would barely be awake. He didn't want to see her now, not at this crucial moment. But he recognised the neediness of her voice, and knew that any encounter would be brief. It was a question of reassurance, for both of them. For Peter to disappear now, or not reply, would simply be mean. And he couldn't do that to his mother.

'Peter, sweetie...are you there?' The request was keener now, with an edge which Peter didn't like. It was the beginning of agitation, and he hated seeing his mother like this.

'Coming Mum,' he sang out, bounding up the stairs. The quicker he got there, the sooner he would be away.

The room was still in darkness, but there was enough light to see his mother turn to him when he squatted beside the bed. He could feel the warmth from the coverings and could see the gossamer threads of his sisters head, submerged below the duvet. There was a sweet sour smell of overnight breath and clammy bodies.

'Are you OK, Son?' she whispered. People said she was beautiful, with her large grey-green eyes, strong nose and skin which hinted of Mediterranean shores, so different to the pasty faces of her school friends, but for Peter she was just his mother, and that alone was sufficient for his love.

'Yes, Mum, I'm fine. I've just had some breakfast.'

'Have you had enough?'

'Yes.'

'Shall I make you some eggs?'

'No, it's alright, Mum, I've had enough.'

'Oh, OK.' Her head had fallen back on to the pillow, one heavy strand of her sandy hair falling across her cheek. 'What are you going to do with yourself today?'

'Don't know, Mum. Might play in the garden. Might go on the bike.'

'Down the road?'

'Might do, Mum.'
'Then be careful.'
'Yes, Mum.'
'Those delivery vehicles go too fast along here.'
'Yes, Mum.'
'Be good, Son.'
'Yes, Mum.'

She closed her eyes and adjusted Julia next to her. Peter bent forward and kissed his mother on the forehead. Her face relaxed and her lips pulled together into a languid, feline smile, and Peter felt glad.

*

The day opened up, but it wasn't inviting. The burden of choice was becoming heavy, nothing like the excitement of the first day of lockdown. Increasingly, he just wanted the comfort of direction. Someone to tell him what to do.

Yet today the choice was clear. Bicycle. His discovery of the Covids' secret, their vicious past, had left him eager and abuzz, with a need to match the discovery with a stimulation of his own. And what better way than eighteen gears of lipstick red speed? A crimson bolt streaking up and down the anonymous asphalt of the private road they lived on. Sometimes Peter wondered why there was not more fuss about his appearance; neighbours gathering to watch, an item on the local news, a visit from the police about strange sightings in the area. But as furiously as he cycled, as blurred as the front hedges and bordered driveways became, as many records set and drag races won, no-one appeared affected by his comings and goings.

Perhaps it wasn't so surprising. After all, he only raced the eastern section of their road, the three hundred metres before the hard surface gave out, becoming muddy twin tracks which only Mr Maguire and his ancient 4x4 used to reach their farm, a further half mile away. Peter had never been that far, the dead end sign at the entrance to the track carried with it a sense of threat, though Peter often looked after Mr Maguire's retreating vehicle, two collies sticking their heads proud of the loose flying canvas flap, and wondered what the farm house, whose chimneys and white roof he could just see, was like.

The other way, the western portion of the private road, had been forbidden him. Its quarter mile led down to the junction of the busy Fassingham Road and, although straight, the depression in the surface a little beyond their house was pronounced, and Peter knew that vehicles rose from there quickly, like malevolent gods from the underworld. 'You wouldn't stand a chance if a van came up there at speed,' his father had explained. Listening in silence to his father's warnings, Peter, too, had come to the conclusion that at the speeds he reached, and even with his braking skills, he'd still be lucky to escape without serious injury.

So he was content to stay along the eastern section; flatter, faster and with only a handful of houses on either side to contend with. In fact, the stretch of road from their house to the end was perfect for his needs. Well, almost. The line was an issue. The line bothered him. He appreciated its contribution to modern living; who could live without electricity? But did it have to be so large to supply the paltry number of consumers further up the road? The thing was the size of a man's heart. It wasn't even a single line. It was concocted of separate strands which had been wrapped together, making it thicker, blacker, more threatening. It was like a coshed towel.

It didn't help that it was on their side of the road, so every time Peter emerged from the driveway, he would first have to see it, then ride underneath. He still couldn't pass below it without flinching, fearing a sudden outpouring of sharp electricity, scragging down to tear at him, roasting him alive, and setting his bike alight. He might manage a final scream, but it would still be abrupt and horrible.

The wooden poles made it worse. Spaced at sixty or seventy yard intervals, the dark snake of wire climbed its way up to the summit of each pole before sloping down again in the centre. On two of the poles, a blackened prostrate figure was being pummelled by electricity. Danger of death. There was nothing subtle about the sign.

Though still early, it was already warm by the time Peter emerged with his bike from the passage which ran along the side of their house. The overnight moisture had evaporated from the tarmac, and in the sky above the rich blue was pushing aside the morning mist. Peter wondered how soon it would be before he removed his sweatshirt. The jogging bottoms flapped comfortably as he slipped quickly beneath the electricity wire and began to ride away from the house. He could feel the air whip into the fabric, caressing his lower legs. Soon, with sufficient speed, he wouldn't even notice this.

He built up speed quickly, and by the time he reached the third pole he was close to his maximum, content now to concentrate on the circular dead end sign which marked the boundary of tarmac and dirt, the point at which, passing the low hedge of the final property he could effect his dramatic manoeuvre, onto the forgiving gravel and mud, pulling and locking the brake, and then looking back admiringly as the rear wheel swept around almost one hundred and eighty degrees, like the arc of a skater, and there he would stop, catching his breath, astounded and thrilled in equal measure, in position to return back towards his house.

The revelation of the Covids had emboldened him and the skid would be proof of that. The faster he approached, the more dramatic the skid. More than just another person to be reckoned with. Passing the second post Peter pushed his legs into even more of a flurry than normal, almost losing control of them, the pistons of a runaway train. It would be a skid to end all skids. He could feel his eyes begin to water from the pressure of the air, his vision clouding.

Then he saw them. Perched on the wire. A dozen he thought, but later realised there could have been fewer. He was going too fast to make such a calculation, and they appeared first as something peripheral, then with greater recognition, understanding and, finally, fear. Covids. Stark against the luminous morning sky. A chord of deadly musical notes, sitting still, waiting maybe for a funeral car to pull by.

Only there was no procession of death, only Peter on his red mountain bike, bearing down on them with a momentum he knew he would be unable to stop before he reached them. It was a brutal trap. They had left him no option. No split second to rethink. He would have to pass them and attempt the dramatic stop he had planned.

But as he began to tense the tips of his fingers around the rear brake lever, the Covids made their move, leaping from the wire, wings spread, the ends like burnt fingers, and shooting off at different angles, some high, some low, some peeling back on themselves, all fleeing into the air with their raucous cackling, part of their attack on him, no doubt. He felt the lurch of the bike at the interface between tarmac and track and, at the same instant, he pulled at the right brake, snapping the rear wheel in its motion.

But something was wrong. He had misjudged. It was the Covids. They had done this. Somehow they had befuddled him, messed him up. They must have, because instead of feeling the aggressive rasp of tyre on dirt drive through his body, Peter found he was no longer upright, the field to his left sliced at an angle that he had never seen before, and then he saw only wide sky, before he felt his shoulder make fierce contact with the ground, knocking the wind from him and throwing the bike beyond his immediate grasp. Even when he felt the fall had reached its conclusion, he waited, eyes closed, unsure if any movement was likely to attract again the attention of the Covids, zeroing in on him to deliver their *coup de grace* or whether, being still, they might view him as already dead, and so not worth the effort. Either way, he had few options. He was hard on the ground, stunned, and a pain around his knee was beginning to grow. Maybe it was better that in these final moments he kept his eyes tightly closed, halfway to oblivion already. Why fight the inevitable? So he waited, waited for the Covids to go about their deadly business. Waited for death.

Chapter 4

'Here, little one, let me help you.'

As he absorbed the voice, Peter opened his eyes. He saw himself close to the ground, his head inches away from the greasy brown mud, tufts of grass, and scattered gravel of the track. There was a dampness in his leg and, looking down the length of his prostrate body, he saw that the limb lay in a shallow puddle in one rut of the lane. The fabric of the tracksuit bottoms was growing dark where the liquid had flowed. The pain was coming from here, too. Before he had a chance to notice any more, a shadow fell across him and the blue sky above disappeared. Then he felt his arm being taken, gripped with the firmness of steel. The world righted itself as he was lifted, doll like, from the floor. Peter let himself be carried, and it was only when he felt both feet firmly on the ground did he allow himself to look.

Before him was a man, but like no man Peter had ever seen before. Where hair should be, there was only material, banded tightly to his head, dirty grey folds which reminded Peter of the damp towels the family used for drying up. And further down, below the stubborn creases on his forehead, below the bushy tufts of grey black brows and proud nose, there appeared the most brilliant white beard, countless filaments falling in waves down the man's face. And, most startling of all, the eyes, bulbous white orbs under sleepy lids, the centre of which were home to the darkest eyes Peter had ever seen. Eyes without pupils. Eyes of a madman, seer, saint or murderer.

The man let go and stepped away from Peter.

'How did you come off?' The voice was deep and strange, and gave Peter no time to think.

'The Covids,' Peter whispered.

'The birds?'

'On the wire.'

'You mean the crows?'

Peter nodded. They seemed to be talking about the same thing. The man looked over his shoulder, up to the now empty line, considering.

'Did they shout at you?'

Peter must have looked surprised and the man continued.

'I mean, did they raise their voices? Was that what caused you to fall off?'

'I'm not sure.'

'They certainly weren't polite by the sounds of it.' Neither the man's tone nor expression changed when he spoke, and he looked coolly and unembarrassed at Peter, examining him. Peter remained rigid, unable to move. Finally, the man turned away, towards where Peter's bike lay in the dirt track.

'Right, let's see what we've got here.' The chain lay limp on the bike frame, and Peter could see that it had detached from the front derailleur. The old man bent slowly, descending to one knee. It was like watching a fairy tale giant, and it took the man several moments to settle. Peter watched as the damp from the ground made its way into the man's thin lilac trousers, though it didn't seem to affect him in any way. The man, back towards the boy, prized the greasy links from between the guides of the derailleur, then lifted the chain back onto the large cog, making sure that it was firmly into the teeth all the way around. Peter felt his terror dissolving, the questions forming. After a while the man began to chuckle, then talk.

'Ha, this reminds me of a bike I had when I was your age. Or maybe a little younger. It wasn't as fancy as this fine model, of course. No gears back then. But the chain kept coming off. My legs seemed to go too fast for the chain to keep up. In fact, I think it used to jump off in protest. I didn't know how to put it back on, either. Cookie had to show me how to do it. Cookie was wonderful with anything mechanical. If it was broke, Cookie could fix it, that's what everyone said.'

He didn't turn around as he spoke, and Peter found himself looking at the man's back, and the light jacket that looked like something from a jumble sale. On his feet, flat bottomed rubber shoes, nautical affairs that could have been hand me downs from a wealthy yacht owner. Once the chain was on the front ring, the man lifted the rear wheel with his left hand and began to spin the pedals. Peter could see the man watching approvingly as the chain first caught on the teeth of the cassette, then began to pull the wheel around, slowly at first, then the spokes soon blurring with speed. Both man and boy shared the happiness of the restored machine. As he rose, one large hand on the handlebar to steady the bike, the man continued speaking. Peter was still not sure who the man was talking to.

'But I did love that bike. It was red too. I had mapped out a special track in the compound, and would hurtle around it, trying to better my previous record, even though I didn't have a watch. Ha, don't think I was flavour of the month with the gardeners though, especially when I'd go off the paths, onto the corners of the grass. Not that they could really complain, not with father being who he was...' And the man stopped, staring away and becoming still. When he turned to face Peter, the man's eyes had lost their former intensity. Now they were just weary.

'There you go, my little daredevil,' said the man, offering Peter the bike. For the first time, the man smiled, the grey ends of his moustache rising like the wings of a gull.

Peter was just about to take it when a voice broke the spell between them.

'Remember your social distancing, Mr Singh.' But instead of turning to where the sound had come from, the man continued smiling at Peter, waiting for him to take the bike, waiting to finish what he had started. Peter, too, was also unable to remove his eyes from the man and his brown parchment face. It was only when Peter had taken hold of one handlebar that the man reacted, letting go of the bicycle and then rising, higher and more commanding than Peter had initially thought, and turned around, back towards the asphalt road, and next to it, the fallow plot of land full of rose briar brambles and long grasses. Standing in the road, close to the field and not ten yards from the pair, stood a woman of middle age, dressed in an orange rain jacket, its matching belt tight around the waist. The woman's hair was pulled back so fiercely that it lay flat on her head, its alternating shades of grey reminding Peter of a bar code. Her face was ashen and in its fleshy depths Peter thought he could distinguish the snaky trails of burst blood veins. Most remarkable of all were her eyes, hard peas behind the magnifying, mustard coloured lenses of her glasses.

'Good morning, Mrs Proudfoot.' The man's voice was strong and official. It reminded Peter of Mr Chambers when he came to speak to their class. It was a voice of authority.

'Mr Singh, are you sure you are not too close to that child? Remember, you should be a minimum of two metres away.'

'Fear not, Mrs Proudfoot. All Government guidelines are being adhered to, I was just…'

'But you're not two metres from him,' she snapped. 'What happens if you've got it, and give it to him? His mother's got a young baby, you know. Babies are in the vulnerable group.'

'As am I, Mrs Proudfoot, as am I. And in a sense, so are we all. All vulnerable. From the very moment we are born. Danger lurks everywhere.'

Peter saw the strained look in the woman's expression and realised why she looked familiar. She had been at their home several times. He had seen his mother share tea and cheap cake with this woman. He remembered how his mother had held him up like a trophy in front of the lady, though the whole encounter had felt strained in some way, and Peter was surprised she had been invited more than once. In reply to her asinine questions, Peter had kept his answers short, and retreated to his room as soon as he was set free. Back then she had appeared in control, enjoying her brief power over the young boy, but now, faced with the unusual man, she was less certain. Maybe sensing her hesitation, the man continued.

'Furthermore, Mrs Proudfoot, I can assure you, that if you look closely at the regulations, as I have, there are exceptions to the two metre rule. One of these, in Section 3 of Appendix B, I believe, covers stricken boys on velocipedes. That's bicycles to you and me. It very clearly states that as a result of fall, or injury to the juvenile, the two metre barrier can be broken. Especially if breath is held tightly. As mine was.'

He paused, and turned to check that Peter was still listening, half smiling before raising his face to the sky where the sun had broken through. The lines on the man's face ran black and deep as gorges.

'But, Mrs Proudfoot,' he continued. 'Feel free to check. Maybe I am confusing it with Section 3.5, which covers young girls tumbling from horses. There are so many regulations. It's difficult to keep up with them, don't you agree, Mrs Proudfoot?'

But the woman knew she was beaten. She could do nothing further. She turned, and without saying a word, stomped back down the road, and both man and boy watched as she went into the grounds of the first house she came to, disappearing into a gap along the brown wooden panelling which ran alongside the road.

But the woman's sudden appearance had broken the invisible link between them, and when Peter turned again and caught the man's eyes keenly fixed on him, all Peter saw was a giant of a man with craggy face and absurd head. All out of proportion, discoloured, uncomfortably different to everything he was familiar with. It was as though he was seeing the man for the first time, and fear began to take hold, and with it flowed the warnings from school. Stranger danger. Beware of people you don't know. Don't let yourself be touched. Don't accept sweets from strangers. Don't take rides from kind unknowns, and certainly, under no circumstances, never, ever, let yourself be rescued from the muddy mire of a bicycle crash...

With barely a look at the man's unsmiling face, Peter grabbed the cycle with both hands, turning and mounting it in one clean movement. His feet quickly found the pedals and he began his flight. But no matter how fast he pedalled, or how much distance he put between himself and the accident, the man's withered, illegible face was at his shoulder the whole way.

He almost fell again when he reached home, the wheels hitting the gravel with such speed that the sudden resistance of the stones caused the bike to jerk and buck alarmingly. He then waited, waited until he could no longer feel the pounding of his heart, and his breathing was his to command once more. Even then he remained still, legs straddling the bike, head half slumped over the handle bars, letting himself take control once more of his body, becoming aware of the pain sliding up from his knee.

Only when a light cloud moved in front of the sun, casting a chill across him did Peter decide it was safe to move. He lay the bike down carefully on the pastel coloured stones and slowly made his way once again to the driveway entrance. Once there, he steadied himself before pushing his head forward, peeping around the corner of the straggly holly bush which served as a kind of boundary fence, and looked back down the road, towards where he had fallen. He could feel himself trembling as he inched his head forward, clear of the tough vanilla leaves, prepared at any moment to whip his head backwards, like a startled tortoise.

But in the distance, where the stranger had stood, there was nothing, and Peter felt relief and bravery returning. He wondered why he had been so terrified. But the smile that he felt forming in response to his silliness never came, because his heart, along with everything else had suddenly been stilled, silenced like a guillotine. For there, above where the road gave out and at the end of the electricity line, the Covids had once more begun to settle. A few initially, but with mounting horror, Peter watched as more began arriving, arriving from all sides, popping out of the bright morning as if by magic, returning to where Peter had first seen them, back to the scene of the ambush, waiting for him again, waiting to finish off what they had started.

Chapter 5

As he arrived for breakfast, Peter didn't need to see the flowing light through the kitchen window to know that the day was already warm. Dressed in just a T-shirt and tracksuit bottoms, he could feel it. His mother's soft singing and easy demeanour was also a sign that the world, despite the virus everyone was still talking about, wasn't wholly changed.

Since his hard fall a few days previously, Peter hadn't returned to his bike, or the lane. He had scarcely been outside at all. To his mother he had related the need for recovery of his heavily grazed knee, but he couldn't fool himself so easily, and the terror he had experienced at the sight of the returned Covids was still close. Would they still be waiting for him on the line? Would they draw closer to attack?

Yet today felt different. The pain in his leg was gone, and he only had the rich scab to casually pick at to remind him of the physical effects of the fall, and three days inside, ensconced with the Eye Pad, had created a barrier with the events of a few days ago. And when he had looked outside, towards the back garden, and beyond that to the folds and fields of the landscape, all the way to the horizon, he knew that his relentless enemies of old would also have been using this time to prepare their next abominable attack on him. Occasionally, he had tried picking them off with a rifle from the safety of his bedroom window, but just as the glass protected him from their weaponry, so too it reduced the effectiveness of his own salvos. He needed to be outside, close up and sweaty against his foes. He needed to be at his HQ.

'Just put some marmalade on, Peter,' his mother said, coming over to him, washing up gloves holding the well done piece of toast firmly in one corner. 'The butter is already on there.'

Peter looked at the crisp piece of toast his mother had placed on the plate to one side of him, before dipping his spoon once more into the cereal bowl. As he munched on the oversized portion he had shoved into his mouth, he watched as his mother returned to the sink, and began to once again sing the intimate song to herself. Her head was high, looking through the kitchen window to the garden beyond, hands automatically fondling the contents of the washing up bowl which she then placed carefully on the drying board to one side. The stark light of the day picked out the dried splash stains on the pane of glass in front of her.

It was part of the family folklore that his mother had a good voice, and had once had aspirations for fame on the back of it. Peter had heard parts of the story before, from various family members, at various times, each instalment overlapping the other and leaving enough of a narrative for Peter to largely understand. It told of a teenage pop duo who had successfully passed a regional audition for a national TV talent show, of both having high hopes of making it through to a live TV appearance before the glitzy gods of the judging panel. But on the eve of the day of travel to the studios in a more glamorous city, one of the pair had fallen ill, not grievously so, only uncomfortably, and as a result the whole expedition had been cancelled, leaving a long trail of 'what if's', and maybe giving rise to the plaintive quality Peter always discerned in his mother's voice.

Whatever the true story, his mother's singing was part of her essence, and for Peter it was always a balm. Listening to her now, the notes rising and falling in careful, controlled modulation, in the warm brightness of the room, Peter felt a deep contentment. It was a moment to be appreciated to the full, a drop of happiness to add to the memory bottle. For such moments are fleeting, and normal life soon returns, as it did now, as from above, Peter heard a floorboard creak. His mother had heard it, too, her voice faltering, and when it started again, something had disappeared, now it was duller, without the spark that had started it in the first place.

The sounds of movement upstairs were bolder now, and Peter knew his father would be moving between bedroom and bathroom, and that his appearance in the kitchen would be a matter of time. Peter ate quicker, milk dribbling from the side of his mouth in his hurry. He wanted to look at his mother, but daren't, and as they heard the regular footfall on the stairs, each thud reduced the volume of his mother's voice. By the time his father opened the door to the kitchen and walked in, the room was silent, and all three of them keenly felt their part in it.

Peter noticed a sheaf of envelopes in his father's hand, the accrual of a week's post he had picked up from the entrance hall table. His father looked glum, or unwell, or a combination of both. Peter could see his mother moving quicker now; static movements around kettle, teapot, cup. It was as though she was preparing a peace offering.

Peter's father took his usual position, sitting opposite Peter, chair pushed away from the table, morosely slitting open each envelope with his finger, clawing at the uneven bits which failed to open neatly. He would pull out a piece of paper, stare at it blankly for a few moments, then either return it to the envelope or fling it aside without a further look. Even when his wife put a steaming cup of tea in front of him, touching him lightly on the shoulder as she did so, still he didn't look up or say anything. He just kept on with the letters.

Finally, he plucked one sheaf from an envelope and looked at it for longer than the others. Peter saw his father's face shift through degrees of interpretation, the end of which it seemed to inflate beyond its natural limits.

'One hundred and eighty quid! For a quarter! That's bloody ridiculous. That can't be right.' His father spoke to no-one in particular and, after a few moments, his mother responded, uncertainly.

'Is it an estimated bill, love?'

'No, it's not. It's one of those smart meter things. That measures your electricity automatically for you.'

'And is it correct?' his mother ventured.

'Of course it's correct,' he thundered. 'I just don't see how we could have used so much electricity.'

'Maybe it's something to do with lockdown, being more time at home,' she said.

Peter avoided looking directly at his father, concentrating hard on lapping up the remnants of milk in his bowl, but he could see his father following his mother with his eyes, watching her silently.

'I know what this is,' his father said. His voice was hard and cold. 'This has got nothing to do with lockdown. This is you and that bloody heater of yours.'

'What do you mean?'

'I mean you and that heater, moving it from room to room, keeping it on all the time.'

'I was just trying to keep warm.'

'But you didn't have to have it on for hours and hours on end, that's just like burning money!'

'But you refused to have the central heating on, so what were we supposed to do?' His mother's defiance was as much habit as principal.

'You'd have ruined us completely if I'd let you have the central heating on.'

'So what were we supposed to do, freeze to death?'

'You were supposed to keep it on until the room is warm, then turn it off. Not keep it on all bloody day.'

'I didn't keep it on all day.'

'That's not what this bill says.'

There was little to be gained from further discussion and all three fell quiet. His mother snapped the radio on, pushing down bitterly on the button, before turning away from the table, towards the sink and window. His father continued staring hard at the same piece of paper. Peter tried to distract himself by listening to the radio. They talked of little else beyond the virus. A further 148 people had died the previous day, rising all the time. Citizens clapping for the NHS. One way routes at supermarkets.

Yet as he listened, his parents bickering slipping away, Peter found his frustration rising. The Covids. No-one was talking about the Covids, these birds, which Peter had seen up close, these avian predators were the real source of the deaths, and yet no mention was given to their black forms, wheeling across the sky in deadly formations. Did they not know about them? Was Peter really the only one on to them? It couldn't be true. It left him confused, and he wondered if he should try to tell his parents about it. But now didn't seem like a good moment, not when he could still feel the crackle of discord in the room. With a glance at his father, Peter slid the slice of toast from the plate, catching it beneath the table. He was glad he hadn't put any topping on it.

'Mum, can I go out to the den?'

'Have you finished your breakfast?'

'Yes, Mum.'

'And the toast I gave you?'

'Yes, Mum.'

She gave Peter a look he didn't fully understand, then relented.

'Make sure you're in shortly to clean your teeth, then.'

'Yes, Mum.'

As he closed the back door behind him, Peter realised his mother could easily have seen the piece of toast he had placed on the ground to thrust his shoes on. But if she had, she must have thought it not worth the argument. Once outside, Peter felt better. He stood still, letting the sun's heat smooth his face. A light breeze was up, catching around the back of his neck and causing the leaves of the ash tree behind the garden shed to shimmer. The noise they produced reminded Peter of the mountain streams they had walked along on a recent holiday. He walked slowly, thoughtfully, down the garden, thinking of everything and nothing; of his parents, of the Covids he might encounter, of his regular enemies, ambushing him right here and now, before he had even taken up a defensive position in his HQ.

He knew, too, he would have to deal with the goal, ten steps from the edge of the slabbed path that ran around the perimeter of the house. The string was still indecently white, a reminder that it had been used just the once. On the very day of its purchase, when Peter had been obliged to join his father at the supermarket, inviting Peter to comment on the choices of goalpost, even though Peter knew his father had already made his decision. Of moving from car to garden immediately on return home. Goals set up, shiny football brought out, and sketchy rules established for the one on one.

The memory of the match that followed still caused Peter pain. He simply couldn't understand why his father was going a hundred percent at everything. No father did that. Real fathers just made a pretence of effort, an encouragement to sons. But Peter's father wasn't pretending. Peter's father was already three goals to the good when Peter said, 'Can we stop now?' 'Stop son? This is time for your comeback. Come on, keep going. Try and get past me!' And though Peter's father had relented a little, scuffing shots and falling over clumsily, Peter was still losing seven goals to four when he complained again. This time his father had responded with anger, doing little to conceal the disappointment he felt from his son's abandonment of the game. Peter's own upset had turned to tears, running inside to be with his mother. Like any son, he didn't like to disappoint his father, he just preferred to be at the other end, in his den. Maybe he should tell his father about the countless, probing attacks he warded off from there, that he was better at finding the mark with the final bullet in the barrel straight to the forehead of a shaggy haired berserker than he was at scoring from the halfway line of a football field. Then his father might understand. But then again, maybe his father might wish to join the defence of the house, and Peter wasn't sure he wanted that.

Once inside his den, Peter felt the reassurance of the tight space, and the gloom was relief from the fierce brightness of the morning. He sat cross legged, his nose almost touching the opening flaps, and ate the dry toast his mother had given him. It was a thrill to eat it outside and, looking at the sparkling seam at the entrance, Peter moved away from the garden, away from Arneby, landing to the side of a mountain, high up between the tree and cloud lines, hiking out, or maybe midway on a mission through enemy lines. They were after him, but soon he would strike camp, and move on again quickly, outrunning his pursuers. Then, once he had handed over the life and death message to the besieged occupants of whereverland, he would have to return, back through the bristling lines of an enemy more determined than ever to capture him, torture him. Maybe worse.

Peter made a final bite into the toast, leaving, as he always did, the thick, unbuttered corner and reaching out one hand beyond the tent and flicking the butt towards the laurel hedge to the side of the garden. He whipped his hand back inside, afraid now that the movement might have been seen, that his habitual enemies, who he had let loose over the last few days, had encroached too close to his den, who were, at this very moment, out there, lying in the wheat field, camouflaged in trees, guns trained upon him. He would have to be careful when emerging. He would have to be ready to fight.

His plans were arrested by the sudden eruption of raucous sounds coming from the laurel hedge. The noise clattered through the small shelter, and Peter froze. Covids. They were here, next to him. He had been too busy fighting invisible enemies when the real danger had managed to get within touching distance of him, and this bellyache of sound emerging from the bush was their battle cry before the final attack. He couldn't move, could only listen in the hope that the old sheets and grease stained grey blankets were enough of a barrier to hide his presence. Slim chance of that, though. The Covids were cunning. Everyone knew that. That's why even adults feared them. That's what all this was about. A real warrior would come out fighting. Was he ready for that?

But as he sat, waiting for his limbs to respond and deciding his next move, the babble continued unchanged. It seemed less threat than quarrelling. The creatures were arguing amongst themselves. Peter wasn't the object of their attentions, it was themselves they were after.

With a bravery that might have been curiosity, Peter moved, thrusting his head from the gap and blinking in response to the sudden flood of light. He turned his head to look at the lime green leaves of the laurel and underneath, in the same position he had seen it last time, was the bird with the yellow beak. Peter smiled in relief as the bird cocked its head and fixed Peter with its pellet eyes. Then the creature returned its attention to the ground, and Peter watched as it made forceful stabbing motions with its beak at the remains of the toast Peter had tossed aside. The corner crust tumbled in the air like a defeated torero on the horns of a bull.

In the light of day, Peter could see that the creature was more dark brown than black and that its breast was lightly mottled, the texture of a watercolour. It certainly wasn't a Covid, and Peter watched closely as the creature abruptly speared the piece with its beak, and almost in one movement, lifted it clear of the ground, flying up with it into the thickness of the foliage. The cacophony from the interior of the hedge rose, and Peter realised that there must be a nest in there, and that what he had discarded as unwanted, was now being shovelled down the gaping throats of hungry little chicks.

Peter held his position on his hands and knees, happy in the sunshine to stare at the hedge, the remorseless chatter from the heart of which allowed him to forget the Covid fear of moments before.

And then the bird dropped again, appearing as if from nowhere, and at the same instant a lull fell upon the hedge. The chicks, no longer hungry, had re-entered their juvenile trance. Peter was surprised to see the mother bird looking at him, breast slightly turned away but one eye intently fixing him. She was still now, with none of the sharp, staccato movements of previously. Peter returned the stare and the silence stretched heavy between them.

'Bbbbbwwwwaaaairtheeeerrrrrccccrrrroooooozzzzz.'

The sound, if even that, was slither slow and heavy, and like nothing Peter had experienced before. It was as if an essence were being dragged from the earth itself, a wave from its deepest core, rising and spreading out, passing through Peter like ripples on a pond. Still the creature didn't move.

'Beeeewairrrtheeeecrowzzzz.'

The wave came again, still syrupy and indistinct, but more urgent, and Peter found himself drawn again to the bird.

'Is that you?' The sound of his own voice surprised Peter. He hadn't meant to speak, and the movement of his mouth felt strange.

'Beeewair the crowzz.'

Like a lens drawing to focus, the communication became clearer, tightening in form and place, pulling itself around the slight creature who stood immobile, barely three metres away, in the half-light under the laurel hedge.

'Are you talking to me? Can you speak?' Peter heard himself say.

'Bewair the crowz.'

There could be no mistaking the words now, and Peter played with them in his mind. Crows. It was the same word the old man had used when talking about the Covids.

Peter looked at the small bird. 'I have to beware of the crows, is that what you're saying?' His voice was agitated and urgent.

'Beware the crows. Beware the crows. Beware the crows.'

The message echoed all around but Peter was sure the bird was responsible for it.

'I understand,' Peter said, offering the slightest assent with his head. The bird looked at Peter for a moment longer, then, satisfied, jerked its head away and leapt backwards, under the shadow of the hedge, before launching itself upwards, into the density of the leaves, and Peter was alone once more.

Chapter 6

Peter withdrew into the darkness of his den and let the unusual experience drain slowly from him. His mind felt tight and hollow at once, and he was unsure how long he remained numb for. But gradually the world returned, and for the first time since lockdown had started, Peter noticed the deep quiet all around him.

The voice. Peter had said he understood, but did he, really? What was it he knew? That Covids and crows were one and the same, and that both must be feared? That wasn't very much. What did they do? How did they kill? Why? And what part did the virus play? The questions arose with urgency and the only thing that Peter was clear about was that the answers wouldn't come to him in the half light of his shelter. He needed help. He needed his Eye Pad.

Peter trotted briskly back up the garden but opened the back door of the house cautiously, half peering around the corner as he clung to the handle. The memory of why he had darted from the kitchen initially was still raw.

His mother was gone, but his father was still at the table, eating a bowl of cereal, silent and staring at the wall ahead. Peter tried a smile as he shuffled quickly past, but didn't check to see if his father had responded in any way. In his hurry to be through, he pulled the door of the kitchen too forcefully, rattling the panes of glass inside the frame. He ran quickly up the stairs, not bothering to close the door to his room, and picked up the Eye Pad. He eased himself into one angle of the bed, tight into the corner wall and deftly inputted his password, before readying himself.

'The...birds...' the words came easily. Both had been prime targets of spelling tests in the past. His finger hovered close to the return button before he stopped. He needed to be clever, like the Covids were. He knew what birds were already. Putting that in by itself wouldn't elicit any useful information. Peter thought back to the words he had heard.

'Beware the crows.' 'You mean the crows?'

As he remembered, the next word became obvious and he began to wave his fingers above the keys. He rehearsed the word in his head, 'K'. Yes, that was definitely the first sound, and it was followed by an 'R'. The 'O' was an easy choice – it was the very heart of the word. After that, he would need to make the word plural, there was more than one of the devils. And though the 'Z' looked as if it should fit, the memory of Ms Parsley came to Peter and he knew that an 'S' must be present somewhere towards the end.

Peter typed. KROS. He screwed up his face. It wasn't right. He didn't know why, just that it wasn't. Something residual from school nagged. Peter looked hard at the word. He was convinced about the first part, there was just something amiss in the second. Something between the last two letters. He tried another 'O' but that wasn't the answer. He looked again at the electronic keyboard, scanning the letters, going through each one to see what might look, and sound, appropriate. He wasn't even sure about the 'W' when he first chose it, but as he looked at the complete word, he knew that he had made the right choice.

'KROWS'. That was it. He was sure. He let his finger fall on the return key in triumph. The screen metamorphosed and Peter read the first line of the results.

Did you mean: The birds, ***Crows***

Peter felt the school shame with the correction and, not for the first time, wondered how he had got it wrong in the first place. Crows. The word looked so correct when written like that. What had he been thinking by using a 'K'?

But the suggestion of video clips to watch was a surprise, and he read their titles slowly. They appeared to be from the same film. Hitchcock.

'Crows attack the students'. 'Crows on the playground'.

He was obviously at the right place. This was clear Covid territory, but did he really want to see the Covids in action? Was his imagination not up to the job? But curiosity was too great, and satisfying it was just a click away. So, he jabbed his finger at the first video.

He wished he hadn't. He wished he had stayed with his own version of the Covids. Not this horror which grew steadily over the next two minutes, time in which he made no effort to use the pause button, to stop the video. And later he couldn't understand why. Why he had continued to watch, from the very first moment, of controlled urgency of the teachers inside the classroom, to the children's sudden running release down the slope, and then to stay, watching and listening, as the children screamed and the crows squealed. The hard, relentless beating of their wings.

It was only when the bloodied and battered girls had reached the safety of the car that Peter threw the Eye Pad onto the duvet, far from him, breathing deeply. He waited a long time, trance like, for his heart to slow and his thoughts to clear.

At least he knew now how the Covids, the crows as they were also known, were killing people. It was the eyes they were after, slicing out the soft greasy tissue and dashing them wherever. Once blind, the victim would no longer be able to defend themselves, and then, just as in the film, the Covids would surround their chosen one, screaming to distract, and using their hard, merciless beaks to puncture flesh, ripping the skin aside as his father had pulled apart the envelopes. Blood, and life, would pour out of the wound. Little wonder that people were concerned about it.

He needed to share the information. Show them that now he understood, saw why people were so scared of this thing. Without a further look at the Eye Pad, Peter bounced from the bed and rushed across the landing to his parents' room. The door was half open and, despite his mounting excitement at the prospect of sharing what he had discovered, Peter slowed, not wanting to disturb his mother. She would still be sensitive after this morning's argument. But as he pushed the door wider, taking care that it didn't knock against the wall, he could see that both sets of curtains were open and the room empty. Peter felt disappointed. He knew any delay in relating the information would reduce the satisfaction of the telling, and the desire to do so. But as he turned to go, a breeze blew in through the top window, catching the muslin curtain. The thin gauze billowed and Peter looked towards it.

For a second time that day, he wished his eyes had been averted. It was a single creature, but even through the muslin veil, there could be no mistaking its shape and where it was looking. Straight towards the house. Straight towards him. In spite of himself, Peter took a few faltering steps towards the curtain, only half believing now that the fabric rendered the person inside invisible. It was as though the single Covid, perched on the electricity line, was drawing him on, like a cartoon traction beam. Peter stopped just short of the window, eyes fixed all the time on the creature who still hadn't moved, still hadn't taken its gaze from him. And then, without any prelude or hint of movement, the creature sprang, leaping from the thick wire with a handful of slow, solid wing beats, leaving the line quivering for a few seconds. But instead of relief, Peter felt his terror grow, for he knew, that not only had the urge to tell someone left him, but that very shortly, the Covid would be communicating with the rest of the group what he had seen. The boy knew their secret. The boy must be taken care of.

*

For what remained of the week, Peter made sure he listened carefully to the news. He would need all the intelligence he could muster. But the reports from the radio were not encouraging. The Covids were sinking their talons ever further into the country, with more cases, more disruption, more deaths, and with each successive calamity Peter reviewed what he had discovered about the Covids, the way they dispatched their victims and his own lucky escape. Above all, he considered what to do about it. That was the key. His response.

But it wasn't easy. Whenever he retired to his den to plan the campaign, the contrast between what he found in the back garden and events in the wider country, only led to confusion. For in its close, safe confines, things had never seemed more right. Velvet blue skies and crystal sunshine greeted him each time he stepped beyond the back door, spring flowers of every hue were starting to appear, and sweet song came from the hedges along each side of the garden. No planes flew overhead, and, when he concentrated hard, Peter realised he could hear no cars, anywhere. His mother had noticed it, too, and one day, when she joined him in the garden with Julia, she said.

'Listen, Peter. Can you hear that?' she raised her index finger to her ear, inviting him to listen. He could hear nothing.

'That's the sound of the earth breathing,' she continued. 'That's what happens when we leave Mother Nature to restore things to how they should be.'

'Oh.'

'It's sweet, isn't it?'

She also gave a name to the bird Peter had 'spoken' with a few days previously. Blackbird. It appeared a little further up the garden, but still close to the hedge, and Peter told his mother he thought he had heard it singing. 'They've got a beautiful voice, haven't they?' she had replied.

And into the silence, all three of them sitting close together on the warm grass, Peter had watched as his mother leant back and turned her face to the sun, an enigmatic smile broadening on her relaxed features.

The Covids were nowhere to be seen, but Peter wasn't fooled. He knew they were out there, waiting, plotting. Midnight black and clever. Waiting for their opportunity. By the end of the week, even his mother had noticed his unease.

'Why don't you go out on your bike today, Peter?' his mother asked as they sat at the breakfast table. Julia was sleeping in the pram next to the table, and occasionally his mother's hand would shoot out into its shadows, easing the child between waking and sleep.

'Nah, I'll be OK in the garden.'

'Are you sure?' His mother's insistence was unusual, and Peter wondered if he should give in to the temptation to tell his mother everything. Then she would understand his reluctance to return to the lane.

'Yes, Mum. I like being in the garden. It's good fun.'

'It's nice when the weather's as good as this.'

'Mmm.'

'It's a pity your father couldn't be here with us to enjoy it,' she said. But the words were more dutiful than truthful, and Peter thought back to the recent weekend, when the weather had been similar, and there had been no suggestion to venture out together.

'Does Daddy have to go to work now?'

'Well, yes and no. Some companies are closing, but Daddy's the boss, and sometimes, in times like these, the bosses have to carry on working, even when everyone else stops, and even...'

But she never completed the sentence, cut short by the shrill ringtone of the phone in the hallway. Despite her flashing smile, Peter could see she was wondering who the caller was. They didn't use the landline much nowadays. Peter watched as his mother pushed the chair back, lifted herself wearily and made a final check on Julia. Then she walked slowly past him, out to the hallway and he heard her pick up the receiver. For a few seconds there was silence. Then his mother spoke, and Peter listened.

'That would be lovely, Mrs Proudfoot...What? This morning?...Well, no, not a problem, no, of course not, I just thought you might mean some other time...I thought the rules were for all households...Well, that's true, and I haven't been anywhere else either, but Steve's seen some people, so he might have got it...so you've seen no-one?...well, yes, of course, Mrs Proudfoot, it would be lovely to see you, I just don't want either of us to get into any bother...yes, if you're sure you think it's safe...oh, OK. See you at ten, then.'

'Mrs Proudfoot is coming around for coffee at ten o'clock,' his mother said flatly when she returned. The conversation had cast a pall over her, and she made no further attempt to continue her talk with him, only reminding Peter to clean his teeth before he went outside as he excused himself from the table. Peter was quick to leave now. He had no wish to be around when Mrs Proudfoot arrived.

He finished his teeth quickly then pulled on the khaki shorts which made him feel like a jungle explorer. Peter soon found himself at the entrance to his den again. The sun was already high enough to cast its rays over the lips of the hedges, falling flat and heavy on the coverings of the den. Peter could almost taste the heat of the interior as he shuffled in on all fours.

His thoughts moved quickly and widely, but he couldn't get beyond the heavy blackness of the Covids. The battle had not been won, and the uncertainty of when and where the fight would be renewed bothered Peter. So, too, the injuries he might sustain. From his regular enemies, he had experienced every type of affliction; bullet in the arm, sword slash to the thigh, gashed forehead. But these injuries rarely left a mark, and the high of his victory always washed away whatever pain remained. But the Covids possessed hyper reality, and the graze around his knee remained stubbornly present, however often he looked. Any more injuries from them were likely to further test his powers of recovery.

Peter was interrupted by the sudden fairy tale song from the adjacent laurel hedge. It was the same as previously. The notes had the freshness of a mountain stream, and without any thought to danger, Peter thrust forwards, out of the shelter. There was the slender blackbird, scraping away with its twig like legs at the dry dust and old leaves beneath the hedge. The creature looked towards Peter, who smiled. The bird held its ground, a few steps from the entrance of the den, and Peter wondered if the creature would speak again, explain to him why it had warned him about the crows, explain...

'Because they are dangerous, of course.'

The interruption was as resonant as it was unexpected and, like the last time, it came from both ground and sky, more significance than sound. It was like the communication of the Gods, and at its centre was the slender mother blackbird.

'What are they going to do?' Peter's own voice sounded clumsy in comparison.

'First they want to do away with you, then they will remove the rest of us birds.'

'Remove you?'

'Remove us. Kill us. They know they can't do so without getting rid of humans first of all.'

'What, all of us?

'Yes, all of you. The Covids know you would do something to protect us. But without you humans, who can stop them?'

'But why do they want to do this?'

'They hate us. Our song, our happiness, it makes them jealous. It annoys them. Reminds them of how ugly they sound themselves. They think of how life would be better for them if we were all gone.'

Peter was quiet, and the voice continued.

'They're clever and they're strong, but you can't have everything in life. Remember what happens if you compare yourself with others, you become vain and bitter. That's what has happened to the Covids. They've forgotten that there will always be someone better, and worse, than them. They've forgotten that.'

Peter didn't know what to say. He thought of everyone he knew, and loved, dying. Mum, Dad, little Julia, Mr Chambers, Grandma and Grandpa Lassiter, Mrs Phillips the dinner lady, James Ancaster and his parents, Akela from Fassingham Cub Group,...

'...even Mrs Proudfoot. Yes, all of them.' Peter wasn't sure where that last sentence had come from and forced himself to look straight at the blackbird. He heard his voice slip as he sought confirmation.

'All dead, for sure?'

'For sure.'

Peter allowed himself a long moment before replying. 'Who else knows?'

'Only you know this, Peter. You are the only one who can hear us, the only one to have come out to us, while all the others stay inside. You must help us, Peter. You.'

Now there could be no equivocation. The task before him was too great. A matter of life and death. For everyone. He must tell someone. Now.

With the urgency of his mission ringing inside him like a tin hammer alarm, Peter ran up the garden. He could see his Mum through the window, at the sink, with something in her hand. She might have smiled at him as he lost her from sight, around the back wall of the house, towards the backdoor. He didn't even attempt to take off his shoes as he flashed the door ajar. He was breathless.

'Mum, Mum, it's the Covids! They want to kill everyone. They want to kill the birds. They want to kill everyone!' Peter heard the echoes of his own voice; too loud, too urgent.

'Sorry, dear?'

'It's the Covids, Mum, they want to take over. They peck out everyone's eyes. Then they kill us, that's how people die.'

Peter realised he was losing an opportunity to clearly present his case. That he would rue this miscalculation later. Still he continued, relentless.

'That's what all this is about, Mum. Older people can't run away like children. That's why they're dying. That's what the Covids are doing.'

'Peter, love, I'm not sure what you're going on about. Covid 19 is a disease, it's a virus.'

'I know that, Mum,' replied Peter without thinking. 'But these Covids are…'

'It's a very serious disease, young man, not a game.' The voice, stern and level, came from the table, behind him, and Peter swung around to look.

It was Mrs Proudfoot. She still hadn't taken off her orange rain jacket, wrapped around her like a boiled sweet. Peter wondered why he hadn't see her when he burst into the room.

'Say hello to Mrs Proudfoot, Peter,' said his mother. There was something restrained, formal even, about the way she spoke. It didn't happen with other friends, and reminded Peter of the class at school being on their best behaviour when Mr Chambers came in.

Peter mumbled a greeting and tried to smile. He kept his gaze lowered but could feel her looking at him with interest.

'What do you think the Covids are, Peter?' Mrs Proudfoot said slowly. The question had a force which alarmed him. He would need to reply carefully.

'I..I was just playing, Mrs Proudfoot. In the garden.' It was a poor explanation for the outburst, but his mother saved him.

'He's always imagining things,' she said, moving across the room, past Peter and setting a pot of coffee on the table. 'If you're going upstairs, love, make sure you take those trainers off.'

'Yes, Mum.'

Peter turned to the door, and with his back towards the ladies, tugged off both shoes without removing the laces. He walked back across the room, around the back of his mother, and then past Mrs Proudfoot. But all the time, despite the fulsome smile, the eyes of the stranger never left him and, as he was at his closest to her, their eyes met, and Peter was shocked to see, behind the sodium tints of the large lenses, not the watery, generous eyes of an old lady, but the coal black, beadlike eyes of another creature, tight and determined. The eyes of a Covid.

Chapter 7

Two days later, Peter still hadn't told anyone, and the impulse to share his secret was stronger than ever. He only asked for a narrow opening, a sympathetic ear. After that, the adults would know what to do. 'Thank you, Peter' they'd say. 'You're a very brave boy, you've done exactly the right thing. We'll take over from here, but rest assured, there's a medal in this for you, a mention on the news, maybe even a meeting with the Queen herself. You will be the toast of a relieved nation.' And then the police would get involved, a hotline to 10 Downing Street and, finally, to finish off the Covids, the army, with machine guns and mortars, would be called in. Peter would, of course, lead them up his street, show them the line upon which the Covids sat and from where they launched their attacks. He might even suggest the best troop deployment.

Only none of it had happened and, as Peter dragged his feet in the baked mud of the path which ran between the fields beyond the rear of their house, he looked ahead at both parents and wondered if now, this Sunday morning, was the right moment.

But once again, he hesitated. He thought back reluctantly to his abortive and flustered initial attempt with his mother. It hadn't been a success, and Peter had spent the last forty eight hours asking himself how he could have done it differently, better, more credibly. But was there anyone else to tell?

Maybe Grandpa Harris and Grandma June? They always seemed keen to humour him. But he would have to do so by phone, and besides, they always seemed to be away at some far flung location, a place which always seemed a little superior to where everyone else was. Nana, Mum's mum, might understand, but she'd want to have a cup of tea and cakes before actually doing anything, and that was a luxury they couldn't afford now. Mr Chambers would certainly know what to do. He was the perfect person to grasp the severity of the situation. But Mr Chambers wasn't at school now, and Peter had no idea where Mr Chambers actually lived, or how to contact him. He could try to visit James Ancaster. James had sometimes helped him take on his enemies across the school fence at playtime. He would understand. But a visit to James meant going in to Arneby, crossing the main road, then taking one of the minor lanes which left the village to the north, roads which Peter had only taken with his mum, and only by car. It would be a momentous trek by bike. It wasn't going to happen.

Which left his father. Peter focussed on the back of his father's narrow head and rehearsed what he was going to say.

But the sudden sound of the bell cut him short, and instead of running to his father, Peter stopped. The sound came from the north, beyond the track which led to Grange Farm, beyond the ripening fields of wheat, and the centre of the village with its rows of houses along the main street, and further, to a narrow lane where the upper boughs of hazels and ash arched across, creating a canopy of permanent shade approaching the church.

It was a single, inarticulate bell, and it took Peter back, two weeks previously, to a normal world, and when just another day at school was being enlivened by a visit to the village church. Peter remembered the children's excitement as they paraded in carefully supervised pairs along the pavement, next to the main road through the village, until the teachers breathed a sigh of relief upon reaching the covered track which led up to the church.

The bell was clanging when they entered the building, causing the pupils to titter and jostle each other even more, but once inside the building was sombre and smelled of centuries. It cast its reverent spell over children and teachers alike and they soon fell quiet. Peter's class were to sit in the choir stalls, close to the altar behind which three panels of stained glass showed the stages of Christ's crucifixion. They waited in silence, while the bell continued to toll insistently.

The boys along the choir row were just beginning to lose their initial inhibitions, starting to kick each other's swinging feet, when the priest bustled in, lanky and indifferent. He placed himself heavily next to Peter, setting out thickly bound books and a coffee stained, hand annotated paper on the pedestal in front of him. Several of his finger nails had dirt trapped beneath, and when he rose to speak Peter caught the smell of the unwashed. Yet his voice was powerful and filled the church. Sitting so close, Peter had felt rocked by the waves of sound as the priest began to explain about the Easter Sunday service they would be rehearsing for.

'And remember children,' the priest boomed, 'the Easter service is the most important service of the whole year. It is the time of our Lord's death, but also his resurrection, his return to life, for us. For all of you. So just remember that, wherever you are, whatever you do in your future lives. Our Lord, all powerful, all benevolent, died for you and your sins.' The priest had paused and Peter could feel the hot breath of his glare as he looked over the heads of the assembled children. Nobody looked up. 'And now, before we sing our final hymn, let us all say the Lord's Prayer together.' The children shuffled, prepared themselves, and the ragged intonation began: 'Our Father, who art in heaven…'

Even before the conclusion of the final hymn, the priest had fled to the vestry, and when the last desultory notes of the song faded away into the church eaves, the bell began its clanging once more, a single monotone that seemed more warning than celebration.

'Come on, Peter, stop dawdling.' It was his father, and Peter realised he had not moved as he listened to the bell, and that both parents had continued without him. Peter could see his father was waiting, maybe impatiently. His mother had gone on, and was heading towards the large electricity pylon which cut across the path. Peter realised that this could be the opportunity to tell that he had been after.

'Coming, Dad,' Peter called. He tried to sound enthusiastic. His father liked enthusiasm. Peter ran up the path, small eddies of dirt turning from each heel strike.

'Sorry, Dad, just listening to the church bell.'

'Huh, is that what it is?'

'It was ringing when we went there for the Easter service practice.'

'Oh.' Peter's parents were not regular churchgoers.

Both father and son turned and began walking. The moment was now.

'Dad?'

'Yes, Son.'

'How long do you think we will have to continue like this?'

'In lockdown?'

'Yes.'

'Dunno.'

'Do you think it would help if we tried to get rid of the crows?'

'Crows, Son? What have they got to do with anything?'

Peter heard the annoyance in his father's voice. Maybe he had been too direct. It was too late though, he would have to continue.

'Yes, if we get rid of the crows, the Covids, then surely this whole thing would be better. People would stop dying.'

'Covid is a virus, Son. It's got nothing to do with birds. It's the disease which is killing people.'

'No, it's not, Dad,' Peter spluttered. 'It's the Covids, I've seen them. They're the ones killing people. We have to stop the Covids, the crows, I mean.'

'And who told you all this, Peter?'

'The blackbird, in the garden, Mum knows which one.'

'Ah, so some of this is your Mum's idea, is it? That would explain things.'

Peter didn't like the way his father said this, and knew he was losing him.

'It's nothing to do with Mum. It's my idea. I mean, I'm the only one who knows about the Covids. But I need to let everyone know. So we can save the world!'

'You sound like you're in a film, Peter,' his father scoffed, then added more kindly. 'But don't worry about such things, lad. Young people are largely immune from it. It's just the older, vulnerable people who are most at risk, so all of us three should be fine. Don't worry.'

Peter was about to explain how the older people couldn't run from the Covids but stopped. They were almost beneath the pylon now, grey and massive, and Peter could already hear the dry hum and crackle coming from its exposed wires. His father wasn't receptive, wasn't even interested. Peter would make no further impression on him. It was as though they had all been tricked, parents, teachers, leaders, all believing this other story. How could this have happened?

He slowed as he drew closer to the metal of the pylon, letting his father move on ahead. Three legs lay in the adjacent field while the fourth encroached onto the path. Before he drew directly under it, Peter looked to either side, and saw similar pylons, higher than several houses, stretching away, far into the distance, beyond sight, the banks of wires looping like orthographical signs in a copy book. It was an invading army, brutal and unwelcome. He edged inside the confines of the feet and stopped. The invisible fizzing from the wires was deafening, forming a prison of sound. He had never remembered it this loud before, and then he realised. Of course he hadn't heard it this acutely before. The metal giants were feeding electricity to houses, along wires like these, along wires like the one which ran down their lane, to houses like his, houses where people had nothing better to do at this time than stay inside and consume that electricity, more and more of it, producing bills which brought men to anger, causing eyes to sparkle with hate and indignation. Peter looked straight up, through the matrix of the galvanised steel, growing dizzy with the sound and the angles and the blue sky which mocked. He could feel himself being sucked in to something, a vortex, and it was only with an effort that was painful, and sense of imminent danger, that he pulled himself free, bursting out, beyond the reach of the pylon, running to catch up with both parents.

*

Peter remained on edge for the rest of the walk, nervously scanning the clear sky for any sign of danger. He felt sure the

Covids would know that he had been unsuccessful in sharing their secret, and that now would be the perfect opportunity to silence him for good, out in the open, where his blood would quickly drain into the parched earth and his body would dry and wither in hours. His parents might not even notice his absence.

But they reached home without further incident and each member of the family was quick to slink off to their own pursuits after the joyless walk.

But time alone did little to quell Peter's agitation, and he was keen to reach his den after lunch. He needed its security to think through the options which remained. He had failed in his mission to tell about the Covids, and thousands, possibly millions, of people around the world would now die as a result. It was a lot for a small boy to bear.

He helped his mother with the drying up, while his father mumbled his excuses and left. Standing side by side, looking out onto the sunlit back garden from the sink and draining board, Peter enjoyed the easy silence with his mother. He almost felt like trying to tell her again. The quiet moment was made for the revelation. But it would be wrong to shatter this bubble of peace. He knew what would happen. He would speak first, then she would question him, growing agitated, sceptical, and then being upset for not believing him, for letting him down. It was like throwing a large rock into still waters. Watching the waves crash on the far shores wasn't what he wanted.

The sun was still high to the south when he returned to the garden. His father was rooting around inside the felt covered shed, and Peter could see his bicycle inside, next to the lawnmower, which his father appeared to be focussing on. Cutting the grass would mean removing the goals, and Peter hoped his father wouldn't see this as an excuse to restart the beautiful game with him. Now, more than ever, he needed to be by himself. If his parents wouldn't help him, he would have to do it by himself. As Peter passed the shed, his father turned, and from the shaded interior offered a half grimace. Peter smiled back, but quickened his pace.

He was reassured to be back in his den, and he sat down cross legged, close to the entrance, and was still. The top beam of the goalpost and material stretched over it was only a few inches above his head. But he liked it this way, small but everything inside its walls was uniquely his, within his control. It was his halo of security, an extension of his self. He closed his eyes and let his mind drift, not forcing anything, letting a solution come to him.

It was only the spluttering of the lawnmower further up the garden which brought him back. With both hands, Peter snatched at the folds of the tent and pushed his head out, twisting around to see what his father was doing. His father held the pull rope of the machine in one hand, and Peter wondered whether the den would have to be removed to allow the grass to be cut. But the lawnmower was no longer making noises, and Peter could see his father settling over the machine with a concerned and frustrated expression. Peter had more time to consider.

It was as he was bringing his head in again that he saw the blackbird. She was standing below the laurel hedge, in her borderland where the dry scrub below the hedge met the lanky garden grass. Her neck was crooked, but she was looking directly at Peter and he felt the weight of her stare. Despite his surprise, Peter glanced back towards his father. But his father was crouched down, absorbed by the failed machine. He would not interrupt them, and Peter turned again to the slight creature whose sharp eyes hadn't left him.

'Did you tell anyone? Did you tell your parents?' The noiseless sound rolled all around him, and for the first time Peter wondered how the creature managed it.

'I tried to, but they wouldn't listen. They didn't believe me!'

'Then you must find someone else to help you.'

'But who?'

'I am not human. I do not know.'

'I've tried everyone I know.'

'Only you can do this, Peter.'

'I know,' Peter said sadly, sinking down in his den. For a moment, the bird was silent. When she spoke again, the waves were softer, lapping at Peter's consciousness.

'The Overlords are getting stronger, you know.'

'The Overlords?'

'The Covids, the crows.'

'Why do you call them Overlords?'

'Millions of years ago, they were Lords of everything and everyone. All creatures obeyed their will. They ruled the earth from the skies. Until new species arrived. Now, they wish to become Overlords again. To regain their power, resurrect their former position in the world, to become masters of all creatures once more. When they have dealt with you humans, then they will turn their attention to us. They have spent many, many years planning their revenge. Now is their moment of return.'

'But that would mean they would have to kill everyone, all humans?'

'Yes.'

'Everyone would die.'

'Yes, Peter, unless you can stop them.'

'I know.'

'And they are getting stronger, Peter. Even your leaders are being attacked. Each day they show less fear, every day they are bolder.'

Peter thought with alarm about the reports that the Prime Minister had been taken to hospital. He hadn't made the connection before, but now the truth of the matter shocked him. Even the most powerful man in the country wasn't safe from the Covids, the Overlords. The situation was getting critical. The sands of time were slipping away. Drastic action was needed.

Peter looked away, towards the bottom of the garden, staring as far as he could see, letting his resolution harden. When he turned back, the bird had gone. But it didn't matter. Peter knew what to do now. He had been too weak previously. He had taken no for an answer when he should have been shriller, more insistent. This time, he wouldn't be fobbed off. He would stand his ground. He pushed his way from the den and began to run up the garden, shouting loudly as he went, 'Dad, dad, dad!'

He couldn't see his father, only the lawnmower in the middle of the lawn, where his father had tried to start it. His bike was also out, lying on its side, just beyond the shadow of the shed. His father must have removed it. The sight of his toy was a shock. It belonged to another world, another time almost, and Peter bent down, next to it, touching the red paintwork, running his finger along the top tube, thinking of the adventures it had given him.

'You were after me, Son?' His father's voice was close, and Peter realised he must have been in the shed, looking for something. His shadow fell over Peter. The moment lasted an instant, but into it time dissolved and Peter found himself again, like before, lying next to his bike, a darkness falling over him, and the vision of the strange old man appeared with a clarity and force which made Peter catch his breath. Of course. The old man who lived up the street. The one who had initially suggested that the crows might have shouted at him. He would understand. Why hadn't Peter thought about him before?

Peter turned to his father, squinting as he looked up into the sun. He no longer thought about confessing to his father.

'Er, nothing, Dad, just wondered why you'd taken my bike out?'

'Just needed a bit of space, that's all. I thought I'd put the spare spark plugs somewhere next to the lawnmower, but I can't seem to find them. You haven't seen them, have you?'

He could have been speaking in a foreign language, and Peter was uninterested. Not now, when his plan of action had become suddenly clear.

'Can I go on it up the road please, Dad?'

'Of course, Son. Just stay up our end. Stop if there are any cars.'

'Yes, Dad.' Peter had already hauled the bike from the floor. He wheeled it quickly around the side passage, emerging at the front of the house. He glanced quickly at the wire and was relieved to see it empty. No Covids would certainly make his mission quicker, but he was prepared to run their gauntlet. There was a sweetness to the relief in knowing what to do, and he was determined not to be deflected from it.

Cycling again felt good, the pleasure of moving faster than walking pace, but as he pulled away and each of the houses he passed grew stranger and stranger, his resolution began to ebb. Was this really the right thing to do?

By the time he saw the low privet hedge which signalled the start of the man's property, Peter was unsure whether to go on. Then he saw the old man himself, filling up a watering can from a tap in front of his house, then turning and shuffling back towards the line of interlinked poles in a patch directly behind the low hedge. The sight of the strange old man held the force of a punch and Peter stopped pedalling and freewheeled towards the house. His hands were poised on the brakes. He could still stop and return back up the lane with his self-respect remaining.

But the bike kept rolling, and the old man looked up and saw him. He didn't smile or attempt a greeting, just followed him with his dark eyes, tracking Peter as he slowed, both converging on a point around the privet hedge. Peter came to a halt and waited.

'Hello, little one, not doing any skids today?' The heavy tone betrayed no emotion.

But Peter couldn't speak. He just sat on the bicycle, shocked and looking in distress at the old man's walnut face, the rough brown in stark contrast to the vivid white of his beard. Peter saw there was fresh dirt on the fabric of both the man's headwear and the gardening gloves he wore.

'Well, have you come up here to see me, or just admire my sweet peas? Or maybe something else?'

Peter realised he either spoke now, or he should never return.

'They're trying to kill all humans,' he blurted. His voice felt distinct from his body. 'They're trying to kill all of us, the Overlords, they're attacking the old people first but once they…'

'Slow, child. Be slow,' the man said calmly, cutting across Peter's gabble. The old man almost offered a smile, and Peter breathed deeply.

Then he told the whole story and the old man listened carefully, occasionally looking down and wiping dirt from the secateurs he had taken from the pocket of his thin lilac trousers. It didn't take long, and when Peter had finished the old man was quiet, looking away, considering.

'So, you're saying that this whole Covid crisis is a plan by the crows, the Overlords as you call them, to kill all humans and then take over the world. To rule again over the remaining creatures, like they once did millions of years ago?'

'Yes, that's right.'

'And you were given this information by a blackbird in your garden?'

'Yes.'

'Young man,' he began, coming closer to the privet hedge, behind which Peter still stood astride his bike. 'What's your name?'

'Peter, Sir,' he said politely.

'Well, Peter-Sir,' and this time the man leaned over the hedge, looking straight towards Peter, his face serious and grim. Peter felt the force of the examination from the man's hard eyes as the seconds ticked by. Finally, the man's lips twitched a fraction and he stroked one side of his moustache, twirling it as he reached the end of the bright bristles. 'If you're right in what you say, this can only mean one thing.' His voice was low and concerned.

'Yes, what?' Peter drew closer to the old man.

'And this must remain strictly between the two of us?'

'Yes.'

'This can only mean…'

'Yes?'

'War!'

Chapter 8

As he spoke, Peter thought he could see the gleam within the dark interior of the man's eyes. It delighted him. The old man understood, had even guessed what they must do next. It was even more than Peter had wanted. The man's face was still close to Peter's and a sharp pungent smell of spicy strangeness came from around the man. It wasn't unpleasant.

'But for the battle to begin,' continued the old man, 'we need the right intelligence. No battle was won without gathering the proper intelligence.'

Peter beamed back. The old man was speaking his language.

'So,' mused the man, looking away from Peter for the first time, 'how do we go about getting that intelligence?'

The question hung in the air, and Peter realised that he might be expected to answer it.

'Well…' Peter started. He tried to sound hopeful.

'Yes, Peter-Sir?'

'Well…er…, I could try asking the blackbird again?'

'Negative,' the old man snapped. 'Negative. Not a sound idea. That is exactly what the Covids will expect. They will be watching you closely from now on. Your blackbird contact is, I'm afraid, a compromised actor. No, Peter-Sir, we must be more discreet, smarter, wiser. The Covids must see and suspect nothing.'

Both man and boy were quiet, falling back to their respective sides of the privet hedge, considering. Peter wondered who would be the first to break the silence.

'Ah, be wise!' cried the old man suddenly, thrusting over the hedge once more, secateurs raised alarmingly. 'That is it! We need to speak to the wise one!'

'The wise one?' said Peter.

'Who is the wisest of all the birds? Which bird did the ancients associate with true sagacity?'

Peter could only raise his eyebrows in enquiry. He wasn't sure what the old man was becoming so animated about.

'The owl, of course! Yes Peter-Sir, I don't know why I didn't think of him earlier. The owl will provide the key to this. I have heard him late at night, from my open window, calling out. Maybe he, too, has been trying to give us warning of these Covids!'

'But how will we know what he is saying?'

'How should I know, Peter-Sir? You are the one who speaks their language, not me.'

'Is it difficult?'

'Was it difficult for you to speak with the blackbird?'

Peter thought for a moment about his conversations with the blackbird. He wasn't sure he knew how he had managed to speak with the creature.

'But when should I do it?'

'The wise one comes out at night, that is all I know. Think about that, Peter-Sir. You will find a way, I'm sure. Report back with the information when you're ready.'

The old man stepped back, and looked around him for the first time. Peter felt a sudden confusion. He had found an ally, but he would still have to fight the battle himself.

'We have been in conference too long,' the man said. 'The Covids may well be observing us right now.'

'But...but...when should I come back?'

'When you have completed the mission.'

'Will it be safe here?'

'Do not worry, Peter-Sir, I will keep an eye on things here. But to be sure, when you are ready with the information, come on your bike, but make sure you are wearing the same green T-shirt you have on today. That will be the sign that you are ready to share the intelligence. And for me...for me...' the old man looked around him hurriedly, his eyes finally settling on the green and white checked gardening gloves he was wearing. 'All is safe if I am wearing these gardening gloves. But should I not have them on, stay away!'

'Yes, Mr...' Peter realised he hadn't even remembered the man's name.

'Singh,' the man offered a half smile. 'The name is Singh. But you can call me Major Singh. That was my name in the army.' And Peter watched as the man lifted himself up from the hedge, pulling his shoulders back, unfurling himself, his chin rising and his aged face shifting to the angle of the sun's rays. Major Singh stood tall and straight, and Peter couldn't have been happier.

'Yes, Major Singh!' cried Peter. He turned the handle bars of the cycle and began to peddle away energetically, his heart filled with a sudden joy, and completely oblivious to the flutter of curtains from Number 20, just across from the Major's house, and the shadow of the viewer pulling itself sharply away from the window.

*

Peter followed dreamily behind his family for the rest of the afternoon, sitting with his father in the living room to watch a film about a retired detective unwillingly brought from retirement for a final job. It was full of glossy violence but there was not a Covid in sight, and Peter didn't really enjoy it. Then, before dinner, his mother drew him into the kitchen and teased him into a few games of Connect 4. He thrilled at her squeal of delight when she saw that she was about to win, rubbing him on the nose and calling him 'Silly Peter' in a way that meant no such thing.

But nothing could ease the heaviness which the fading light of evening was bringing. Speaking with the owl had seemed straightforward when Major Singh had given the order, but now it was less clear. Peter had no inkling of where the owl lived, and if the owl only made his appearance at night, how was Peter to get out of the house at such a late hour without his parents finding out. It was impossible. Peter wasn't even sure he'd be able to communicate with the owl once located.

He kissed his father goodnight in the living room then trudged upstairs to wait for his mother. He got into bed reluctantly, the plan that he had spent all afternoon thinking about, and dismissing, was still the best one he had.

'Good night, love.' He felt his mother's kiss on his forehead, and made a snatched attempt to return the gesture, and then his mother closed the door behind her, throwing the room into almost complete gloom. Peter waited until he heard his mother's steps on the stairs and then moved, pushing the duvet back, and bouncing forwards on the bed before pulling the latch handle which allowed the double glazed panel to be pushed open. The cool night air felt alien to the room. When he looked out into the garden, he could see very little, only the blacker outlines of the uppermost branches of the ash tree. But of the garden itself, and beyond that, the fields and hedgerows of the far lands, he could make out nothing.

The night was still, with just the occasional burst of flutter and rustle as the wind caught the garden foliage. A couple of times, he heard the rise and fall of vehicles passing the front of the house. Of the owl, there was no sound, and after listening intently for a while, Peter fell back onto his bed, growing sleepy and unsure. He closed his eyes and considered. Maybe the owl was speaking, but Peter just couldn't hear? Or maybe it was just too early – didn't Major Singh say that the owl came out late? Or maybe Peter was listening in the wrong direction. The window of his room faced out towards the back garden, towards the south, away from the electricity line, the road and where Peter had spoken with the major.

When he next became aware, he found he was cold, only half covered by the duvet, and the window was letting in a stream of cold, uncomfortable air. He shut it and lay back, listening now for the sounds of the house instead. But all was silent, and under the door the main landing light was off. He realised his parents must already be in bed and that he had spent several hours asleep instead of listening for the owl. Maybe the owl had spoken during his slumber, the message given, but not heard. Peter felt a rising anger and frustration. His first mission, and he had disobeyed orders, falling asleep at his post, the worst dereliction of duty. He wouldn't find it acceptable amongst his own troops. What would Major Singh say? How would it affect their campaign? He would need to be bold to make up for this lapse.

He slipped from the duvet and, without putting on any slippers, padded carefully across the carpeted floor, inching the door handle down slowly, stopping at every metallic protest the mechanism gave out, until he finally felt the latch free from its casing. Then he pulled the door open and tip-toed onto the landing. He felt exposed by the thin gleam of the night light from the wall. The spare room was next to his and gave out on to the front of the house. It was to be Julia's when older, but while the baby still slept with her parents it was empty, except for the made bed and adjacent chest of drawers. Peter repeated the exacting process of the door handle and was soon inside the empty room. He closed the door carefully, but didn't turn on the light.

The room felt sterile and cold, and the curtains were wide open and precise. He would be in trouble now if caught. The window had the same mechanism as his room and he quickly opened it, peering intently out into the night sky in the hope that it would help him hear better, too. But the night was still, and even the wire, whose blackness could be made out against the night sky, seemed less malevolent. Kneeling on the far end of the bed, Peter found he could place his elbows on the windowsill, his face between the gap of the opened window. He listened for a few minutes, but there was nothing beyond night scratchings and the faraway acceleration of a motorbike. It wasn't comfortable, and Peter could feel himself becoming drowsy once again, his powers of concentration tiring him more than he had expected. After a while, he relented. He didn't need to be propped against the window to hear, he could easily get under the covers of the duvet and lie down but still keep alert for the sound of the owl. So he pulled himself back from the windowsill, pushing the window open wider, to ensure he missed nothing, and then lay down, pulling the duvet up, over his legs, chest, closing his eyes to better concentrate on the sound.

And so Peter lay, losing himself in time once again, and as he listened, from the swirl of silence, a steady buzzing began, low at first, then more insistent, something novel and yet also something remembered. And into the fizz and crackle, maybe in front of it, maybe behind, came the distinct cry of an owl. 'To-wit to-whoo, To-wit to-whoo. To-wit to-whoo.' A steady, pulse like call that melded with the hot static, all of it entering him. And when it was inside, he felt the melange turning around gradually and methodically, like clothes in a washing machine, churning and tumbling down on each other. Around and around. Slow, turgid revolutions, like the quiet accumulation of dusty gases in space, swirling around at high temperature, until one day, the gas and dust is burned away to reveal a most brilliant, powerful star, forged white hot in its midst.

'Peter, Peter, love, what are you doing here? Are you OK?'

Peter wasn't sure which was more of a surprise, the sudden appearance of his mother or the fierce light which streamed in from the open window. He didn't know where or when either had come from. Peter feigned sleepiness, knowing that after the concern would come the accusations, especially if his father was aware of the transgression. But he wasn't thinking about that. It wasn't important, not now, not when he had discovered the information he had been sent to find out. Mission accomplished. The answers were all in his head, and all that mattered now was telling the major.

Chapter 9

Peter was the first one down to the kitchen, and in his agitation considered making a break for it, before either parent slowed him with breakfast obligations. He wasn't scared that he would forget the information he had gleaned during the night, only that delay might be costly. For humanity. But before he could act on the impulse, the glass door of the kitchen swung open and his father trudged in.

'What are you doing up so early?' his father said. He seemed put out by Peter's presence.

'Just hungry, Dad.'

His father made a strange noise in his throat, but moved past the table, towards the sink. There he stood in silence, looking without seeing through the window as the water from the tap gushed into the kettle he had picked up. The sound of the filling water masked his mother's entrance, and it was only when Peter's father turned off the tap that the Peter became aware that all three of them were in the room. The silence grew gradually louder, and Peter wished the radio was on. His father returned to the table, where Peter was already serving himself, tipping up the cereal box and letting the dry flakes tumble out. When he had finished, his father reached across, picked up the same box, and repeated Peter's actions. His mother busied herself around the sink and worktop, and Peter could see her opening cupboards, taking things out, leaving them in no particular order on the worktop; marmalade jar, sugar bowl, tea pot, vitamin bottles. Knives and spoons from the cutlery drawer. In a short while she would begin transferring them all to the main table in the centre of the room. He wondered which parent was going to speak first, though the rising murmur from the heating kettle was a protection of sorts. Following its crescendo, it died away quickly and Peter felt the absence of sound as something physical.

'Do you really have to go today?' It was his mother. The words emerged hurriedly, as though they'd been straining to come out. Peter's father let the question hang for a cruel moment.

'I've got some cards to print for a company, and I'm also expecting those Perspex sheets in today.'

'But I thought you said things had dried up?'

'There's still things to do, Donna,' his father said wearily. 'I'm by myself, remember.'

'Can't you get one of the others to come in?'

'They're all on furlough now. It would be illegal to get them in.'

'Why don't you just work half day then?'

'I can't, Donna, love. I need to work a bit later tonight.'

Peter saw his mother stop what she was doing. One hand cupped a pot of Marmite tight to the work surface. She turned her head and looked straight towards her husband who continued to calmly eat his cereal.

'You didn't tell me you were going to be late.'

'Sorry, love, I thought I'd mentioned it. I need to make an international call. It's in a different time zone.'

'Can't you call from home?'

'I'd prefer to call from the office. Quieter. Can concentrate better.'

His mother stared rigid towards the table but her husband continued to shovel heaped spoonfuls of cereal into his mouth, not daring, wanting, to return her gaze. Her eyes narrowed and her lips tightened. It was an unnatural expression.

But whatever violent eruption lay behind the expression never came as Peter, whose concentration had been monopolised by the conversation between his parents, failed to swallow properly, the soggy cereals catching somewhere in his throat and causing him to first cough, then splutter, and finally eject in an inarticulate cloud, the offending mixture of milk and mushy corn. Drops of it reached his father's hands on the far side of the table, but most of it fell on the assorted pile of old envelopes, instructions for medicines and gutted candle in the centre.

Peter's father looked up in surprise and disgust, but his mother was over to him in an instant, patting his back, before he felt her arm draw around his shoulder. Whatever she had been on the point of saying was forgotten.

'Are you OK, Peter?'

Peter wasn't sure if something was still trapped in his larynx and stayed quiet. He could feel his eyes teary from the tumult of the expulsion.

'Here,' his mother continued. 'Have some water.'

And Peter found before him a glass of water, magicked from somewhere. He drunk and felt the relief of clearing passageways, blood slowly draining from his flushed face. He was grateful for his mother's close presence and smile, a smile that could stay with a little boy for a lifetime.

Shortly after, his father slipped away wordlessly. Peter felt his own excitement returning, filling the space that the tension in the room had occupied. He began to think again how he would phrase the news to the major. He needed to be away. Right now.

'It's still very early, love,' his mother protested when Peter requested permission to go up the lane.

'Ah, Mum, but I really want to go out on my bike,' he whined.

'Just wait till nine o'clock, love.' Her voice was soft, but Peter knew better than to push the matter. Besides, he could see, as she sat down and joined him at the breakfast table, taking modest bites from the thin toast and gazing without emotion at the empty wall in front of her, she had other things on her mind. Instead, Peter looked the other way, towards the clock above the window which gave out to the rear garden. It wouldn't go fast enough. The hands moved ponderously, like an old man in a movie.

The radio was on now but provided little relief. The number of cases across the Atlantic was rising, while in the UK, the Covids had now killed over 5,000 people. As he sat, tapping his foot in anticipation of moving, Peter tried to imagine what 5,000 people would look like, all together in a big field, hemmed in by invisible barriers and waiting in mute anticipation of their fate, whilst from above a dark cloud of Covids slowly descended, their wide ugly calls becoming louder as they suffocated the light from the sun with their overlapping wings. Then they would fall on the helpless human mass, seething and writhing and eventually fusing into one mess. A sloppy soup of blood, guts and bobbing eyeballs.

'Peter, you'll need something warmer than just that T-shirt,' his mother said as Peter jumped up from the table and hurried to the back door, pulling at the handle even before the last pips to mark the arrival of the new hour had completed. He held it open with one hand, balancing himself, while with the other he stuffed a foot into each trainer.

'Ah, Mum, it's not that cold outside.'

'Either you get a top, or you're not going out, Peter.'

The delay was momentary, though Peter knew that at some point along the lane, safe from the vigilant eyes of his mother, he would have to strip himself of the navy top he had rushed upstairs to retrieve, leaving on the agreed T-shirt. He didn't want to mess up by not giving the correct signal.

There was no one else on the lane and, after stopping to remove the top, he quickly built up speed before pulling on the brakes carefully when he approached the old man's house. He had already planned what he would do. Ride slowly, parallel to the hedge, allowing the major plenty of time to see him, though he suspected that the Major, appreciating the importance of his mission, would be out in an instant.

But there was no sign of any movement at the property, and by the time Peter reached the beginning of the dirt track which led to Grange Farm, he had slowed to such an extent that he had trouble keeping upright. When the tarmac ran out, he put his foot down and looked keenly at the building. It was a long, low slung house which might once have been a humble cottage, but whose whitewashed frontage was now marked by lines of haphazard brick courses, showing the slow accretion of centuries. Peter stared hard, as if by force of will he could squeeze some reaction from the lifeless building. But the house continued inert, its dark windows like closed eyelids. Peter considered forcing the issue. There was no gate, and he was now close to the stony driveway which curved around, ending at the front door. Would knocking at that door be initiative, or disobedience?

But Peter hung back, recognising his own impatience. The major had told him the signal, and Peter had agreed. There was no good reason to break with orders so soon. And besides, perhaps the major was engaged on another operation, maybe even taking on the Covids at some other place? Peter hoisted himself onto the saddle again, and retraced his way along the front of the property, turning the pedals so slowly it became difficult to ride, and trying to make himself as tall as possible – he didn't want the major to miss the agreed signal. All the time his eyes scanned the house for any slight movement.

But by the time he reached the end of the hedge and the line of tall trees which acted as a border to the next property, nothing had changed, and for the first time he began to feel conscious of where he was, what he was doing, and how his actions might be seen by others. They weren't the actions of a boy lost in play. Immediately opposite the Major's house, the oblong parcel of land had been left to wild grasses, but the adjoining plot had been developed, split into two, with Mrs Proudfoot's at the front, surrounded on all sides by a featureless fence, while to one side, a gravel path led to the rear, where another house stood, only the roof, chimney and satellite antennae of which could be seen from the road.

Peter looked apprehensively towards Mrs Proudfoot's house. Above the prison panels of the fence, a generous section of bay window could be discerned. A muslin curtain screened anything of the interior, but it made Peter feel vulnerable, and he thought back to his previous encounter with the lady. She could be watching him even now. He simply wouldn't know.

Peter turned back to the major's house and took a deep breath. He would try once more, and if not successful, then...But Peter didn't want to consider that prospect, not just yet.

It was as he was halfway along the privet hedge that Peter saw the first sign of movement. Nothing more than a shadow, fleeting behind a window close to the front door of the house. Peter pulled hard at the brakes and watched as the front door slowly opened and the bearded head of the old man emerged. He raised his hand in recognition of Peter, and in his excitement and surprise, Peter found that he had acknowledged the salute by raising his own hand. Yet the man looked different this morning, frail and without the energy that Peter had taken from the previous day, and Peter watched with mounting dismay as the old man shuffled along the driveway, out towards him, approaching as if to put out the recycling bin or some other mundane task.

On his feet he wore slippers, whilst wrapped around him a checked dressing gown of coarse material that reached to his ankles, tied at the waste with a stretch of curtain pull rope with tassels at each end. On his head, instead of the precise folds of the previous day, the man had clumsily placed a black woollen hat. It bulged awkwardly, wisps of silver hair pushing from beneath its hem. He looked sleepy and lost, and Peter was confused at the disappointment he felt.

It was only when the major was a few metres away that Peter realised what he had missed in his examination. The gloves. The signal. The old man's hands were bare. Peter looked on with horror, transfixed, and unsure of what to do, run, as the Major had instructed, or stay and wait for an explanation. But he couldn't move, only stare, as the old man, too, became aware of the boy's distress, catching Peter's gaze and looking down at his hands. He stopped a few metres from the boy, thinking hard, remembering.

'Ah, my gloves! Yes, of course, the signal, of course…how silly of me.' He looked up, his eyes now bright and alert, scanning the boy. 'But don't worry Peter-Sir. All is well. It is safe. Just the forgetfulness of an old man. Don't be alarmed!' He smiled at the boy for the first time, his eyes narrowing, crow's feet deepening at each temple.

'But you have done well, little one, remembering our signal. A good soldier.'

Peter beamed back, and he could feel himself swelling with pride. Any misgivings fell away in his relief, and Peter was quick to begin his narrative.

'I did it, Major Singh! I stayed awake and listened to the wise owl. I heard her in the night.'

'And what did she say, little one?'

'It's the wires! The Covids are getting their power from the wires they sit on. That's what is making them so strong, so powerful right now. Everyone is staying at home and using electricity, and all that electricity is flowing through the wires and being sucked up by the Covids!'

The old man's eyes hadn't left Peter's excited face for a moment, and their burning brightness only served to encourage Peter more.

'It's making them stronger, and more aggressive. You've seen the look in their eyes when they're on the line.'

'Mean and fierce?' said the old man.

'Yes.'

'Without pity?'

'Yes.'

'And you say the electricity is somehow passing through these Covids, giving them the extra strength, to attack us humans, to pluck our eyes and blind us, then rake us to death with their claws?'

'That's what the owl said.'

'So,' mused the old man, looking away from Peter and up to the empty wire, 'they're not just normal overlords, but electric overlords?'

'Yes, Major Singh,' cried Peter. 'That's exactly right. They're electric overlords!'

'Hmm,' the old man paused, letting the long white strands of his beard slip through his fingers. 'Then it is worse than I originally thought,' he finally said. 'Far worse.'

For a long while, Peter was quiet, letting the old man think, waiting for him to reach his conclusions. He waited until he could bear it no longer.

'What are we going to do then, Major Singh?'

Peter looked eagerly up at the old man who still had a faraway look in his velvet eyes, as if Peter's question had taken him further back, to some remote place deep in the folds of time. And then, with the faintest puckering of his lips which might have been the choked beginnings of a smile, the old man bent down close to Peter, so close that Peter could feel the heat of his morning breath, see the smoky pores of his parched skin.

'We need to remove the birds from the line, Peter-Sir. We need to deprive them of their power. We must declare war on the Electric Overlords.'

'But what about all the other Covids? Around the rest of the country? How will we remove them all?'

'We don't, Peter-Sir. The Covids are not daft, as soon as we banish these ones here from our line, their fear will be infectious, they will know we have the measure of them, they will all surrender, go back to their previous lives. Cease their overlord status. Of this I have no doubt. But we must get them off this line, here, me and you. After that, they will all capitulate like falling dominoes.'

The boy held the old man's fevered gaze, returning it with an ardour of his own, ecstatic at the major's certainty. Only slowly did Peter emerge from the fog of his excitement, the implications of the major's strategy trickling down, making him doubt for the first time. It must have shown on his face, because he was relieved rather than alarmed when he felt the major's hand, hard and serious, fold over his, holding it tight to the handlebar. It meant he had total confidence in what the major said next.

'But don't worry, little Peter-Sir. There are ways to do this. Come back early this afternoon. I have an idea I want to try.'

'Yes, Sir.'

'Good boy. Brave soldier!'

'Thank you, Sir!'

'Everything, Peter-Sir, will be alright. Together we will save the world!'

'Yes, Sir!'

Chapter 10

Peter didn't stay long at home. Just time enough to plead an early lunch and give a distracted greeting to his baby sister, whose finger pinches and unalloyed smiles filled him with joy, but were not enough to get beyond his fevered speculation of what Major Singh's battle plans were.

For a brief while he tried his den, but as he sat in the soup warm gloom of the closed interior, no new battles came to him, and neither was there any sign of the blackbird now, and even if there had been, Peter wondered if she would even speak to him. So he retreated cautiously to the house, going upstairs and using the dead time before lunch to take stock from the safety of his bedroom window, looking out over the back garden, body tightening when he thought he saw a Covid scrag into view.

His mother seemed distracted when he did go downstairs, rushing between stations to prepare him the cheese on toast, but still getting things in the wrong order, then trying to make up for it with renewed haste. Peter silently pleaded for calmness. When he had finished eating and was eager to leave, she pulled him close, constricting his arms.

'I love you, Peter,' she said, leaving a powerful, lingering kiss on his head. She was almost on the point of tears. But it was not something he could worry about, not when he was on the point of potentially saving all humanity.

Peter still had to wait a few moments at the mouth of the driveway before Major Singh appeared, hurriedly from the far side of the house, walking on the concrete pathway surrounding the building. He silently hailed Peter to come forward, onto the stone driveway, towards the house. Once beyond the threshold of the property, Peter suddenly felt self-conscious, as though he had broken some taboo.

Major Singh had changed clothes, and now resembled how Peter had first seen him, the flat rubber soled shoes, lightweight and creased trousers, and a dirty mustard coloured jacket. His hair was hidden, coiled up Peter imagined into the sharp, black folds erected high on his head like a sultan's palace. The whole effect was more comfort than battle, but Peter was too excited to care.

'Are you ready then, Peter-Sir?'

'Yes, Major Singh,' cried Peter, propping his cycle against the side of the house, the handlebars resting close to the external tap.

'Well,' he began, stooping towards Peter, his eyes opening wider. 'My plan is this. We wait for the Covids to come. Then, once they're on the line, we're going to turn off the electricity, dry up their power supply. Without the juice to feed them, they'll no longer be overlords, just normal birds, maybe not even that.'

Peter looked at the lively features of the old man. He loved his earnest enthusiasm, and waited for him to continue.

'I'll go around to the back, flip the switch on the supply box, and that will turn the line dead. You stay and watch what happens.'

'Are you sure it will work?' Peter asked.

'Yes.'

'What about all the other houses?'

'Well, I can't guarantee that it will work all the way along here, but remember what I said about dominoes. We have to start the rot from somewhere, and once we blitz this part of the wire, the message will soon travel to the other parts, as fast as electricity itself. Remember, small actions can make a big difference.'

'Er, yes, Major Singh.'

'But first we must wait for the Covids. Come, we can sit here, prop our backs up against the house.'

'But won't the Covids see us?'

'Ah, you are quick, little one. I can see that one day you will make a great general. And it is for that reason, I have brought this around.'

Major Singh turned smartly, walked along the path and disappeared around the corner of the building. He returned immediately, shuffling along with a large panel of slatted wood. Some of the slats had jagged holes in them, and one side was missing the thicker runs which held the slats in place.

'This is one of the broken fence panels,' explained Major Singh as he let the sheet down, one side resting on the concrete path. Then Major Singh returned to the corner of the house, this time picking up what looked like an old fashioned metallic bin, the sort Peter had seen in old cartoons, except this had a small funnel in the centre of the lid. The object hadn't been there on his previous visits.

'Right,' grunted the major as he picked the object up by its handles and worked it across to where Peter was still standing on the path, 'all we have to do is prop the panel on the burner and that should screen us from the Covids. What do you think?'

The old man had left the tin burner on the path and then hoisted one end of the panel onto it. He adjusted the burner, bringing the whole crude shield closer to the house. It was makeshift and unimpressive.

'There, sit down there, against the wall, you can still see above the panel, yes?'

Peter sat down in the gap between the wall and the panel. Much of the garden was now blocked from view, but there was a clear line of sight to the thick cable running high above the hedge line.

'Now we must wait for the Covids to come before we turn off the electricity,' said the major, settling down next to Peter. He copied Peter's position of back against the wall, forearms resting on drawn up knees. He didn't appear comfortable. Peter looked again across the front garden, towards the line.

'But won't the Covids still be able to see us? I mean, if we can see them, surely they can see us?'

'Well, yes, we're not completely hidden, but they will only see our heads, not the rest of us.'

'But I thought you said the Covids are clever. Won't they notice us?'

'That is a risk we will have to take.'

'Wouldn't it be better if we go inside, Major Singh?'

'Er, no, Peter-Sir.' Major Singh looked pained. 'I don't think that is a good idea. Best be out in the open. Seeing the enemy up close, eyeball to eyeball, then they'll see we're not scared of them.'

After that, both of them were quiet, concentrating on the empty wire, an ugly scar across the virgin blue of the sky. Peter hoped his mother wasn't missing him. He had said he was going into his den, hadn't mentioned the lane. If she went to the window she would see he wasn't roaming around the garden, charging to the brink of his territory at the field, seeing off his enemies. He wondered if he should return.

But he liked sitting here with Mr Singh. Brothers in arms. Steeling themselves for the battle to come.

'Where do you think they are?' Peter whispered after they had sat in silence a while. He was beginning to feel restless. 'Why aren't they coming?'

'I don't know.'

'Maybe the Covids are busy attacking other people, in other parts of the country?'

'Maybe, but I think they'll be back here soon.'

'They've attacked Mr Johnson again. He's got worse in hospital. I don't know how they did it, because he's the Prime Minister, he's the most powerful person we have. If they can get him, they can get anyone, can't they?'

'The Electric Overlords are clever, for sure.' Mr Singh was quiet for a moment. 'Do you know of anyone else who has been attacked by the Covids, Peter-Sir?'

'Do I know of anyone?' Peter wasn't sure he understood the major.

'Yes.'

'No, I don't think so. But the radio said that thousands of people have died.'

'Yes, I have heard the same.' Again, Major Singh grew quiet, his eyes still focussed on the line twenty paces across the garden. 'But like you, Peter-Sir, I know of no-one who has caught this...been attacked by the Overlords.'

'No.'

'All we hear is that the Covids are a great, unseen danger which we must guard against and be fearful of. Are you scared, Peter-Sir?'

'Yes, I think so, Major Singh. I've seen a Covid. I've seen what they can do.'

The old man ignored Peter and continued. 'An American president, I've forgotten which one, once said a wise thing about fear. He said that the only thing to fear is fear itself. Do you know what that means?'

Peter didn't, and waited for the old man to continue.

'It means we shouldn't let things scare us more than they need to.'

'But the Overlords are trying to take over the world. We must be scared. They are killing people.'

'Have you seen the dead?'

'No, but everyone says that lots of people are dying.'

'Neither have I seen the dead, Peter-Sir,' said Major Singh, speaking more to himself. 'Even on the television. We see hospitals, tubes, medical machines, trolleys, blurred faces, but death itself?'

Peter turned to the old man. He wasn't sure he understood Major Singh.

'Keep looking at the wire, Peter-Sir. We don't want to miss the Covids when they come. We need to pull that switch as soon as we get a decent number on that line, remember that.'

Peter returned his gaze to the dark cord. Against the calm of the blue sky and the day's warmth it seemed impossible that anything evil could appear.

'Of course,' Major Singh was speaking again, 'these Overlords are a terrible thing, I'm sure, and we must take every precaution against them, as we are doing, Peter-Sir.' The man paused, reflecting. 'But when I was younger, younger than you even, one time I had to walk a long way, a difficult journey, on foot, behind a cart. For a whole week we walked. And in that cart, we had to pack everything we owned, everything we could take, had time to take. And I saw things on that trip that I hope never to see again, bodies, hundreds of bodies, mutilated, bloated, burnt, rotted. That was death, but close up.'

'Was that the Covids?'

'No, little one,' the man chuckled. 'That had nothing to do with the Covids. That was just man's justice to man. Or injustice. When you see death like that, what is happening now is less…less…' and the man turned to Peter, smiling as if enjoying a private joke. 'Well, let's just say I can't take this lockdown quite as seriously as others.'

'But isn't it better to be inside our houses, to be safe from the Covids?'

'Oh yes, Peter-Sir, for sure, who could argue against being safe? Especially from these Covids. They're deadly, as you know. A Government's first duty is the safety and security of its citizens. Of course, let's keep safe where we can.' He paused, looking away. 'I just wonder what is being lost as a result of us all hiding away inside.'

Peter looked at the old man, his eyes wide in enquiry.

'I'm thinking of you, Peter-Sir,' the man said by way of explanation. 'I'm thinking of you, unable to run amok and play with your friends, I'm thinking of your teachers, removed from your energies and the quiet satisfactions you give them every day, I'm thinking of church goers cut off from the source of their faith, and fathers and mothers who will lose their jobs because no-one is buying what they are selling, and wondering which pile of savings to run down in order to make ends meet. I'm thinking of all those poor old people in care homes who will die without any family to be with them. That is terrible, absolutely terrible. I'm thinking, Peter-Sir, of all those lovely smiles lost behind surgical masks and all those magical moments when people get together that will never be. We're all wilting a little bit more with each dawn, and no-one is adding all that up, no-one is putting that disruption onto the other side of the scales.'

'How would you weigh that anyway?' Peter was surprised at himself. It was a good question, a worthy question, and he felt the old man looking down on him curiously, the twitch of a lip causing his moustache to ripple. His eyes narrowed and focussed on Peter. When he spoke again, he began slowly.

'Ah, now there is a question, Peter-Sir,' he said, each word heavy with careful enunciation. 'You would indeed need a big set of scales for that equation, and I fear it would be impossible to do. How to weigh one life against another? I don't know. All I know is that we shouldn't be afraid of death, especially us old ones, who've seen a lifetime of sunrises and sunsets, and travelled to many new lands. Often we hold on to life out of force of habit, not because we want anything more from this world. But you little ones. You are having it rough. Each new day brings something new for you...'

It was at that moment the first Covids appeared, seemingly emerging from the background of the sky itself, circling high at first, then lower, tracing a black vortex until half a dozen fell onto the line at the same time, all facing the house. Peter couldn't move.

'Sshhh, stay here, Peter-Sir,' whispered Major Singh, easing himself up from the hard concrete with a sound like gas escaping from a fizzy drink. 'I will turn off the electricity. Be prepared for action.'

Peter felt, rather than saw, Major Singh slip noiselessly around the corner of the building, and as he disappeared from view, one of the Covids released a long cry, high and defiant into the sky. Peter felt it run through every pore of his body. He was terrified. The Covids were very black and very real, and he doubted his standard armoury would be of any use now.

'Did it work?' Peter hadn't noticed the old man return, but there he was, barely six inches away, expectant and awaiting Peter's report. The man's forehead had a faint patina of sweat, shiny and translucent like fresh paint.

'Did what work?' Peter replied, puzzled at the question.

'The electricity! I switched the electricity off. Did it work? Did anything happen?'

Peter looked in alarm from the excited face of the old man towards the line where the Covids still sat, fanned out, waiting. If anything, their numbers seemed to have swelled.

'They're still there,' said Peter. 'I don't think anything happened.'

The old man looked hard at the boy, as if deciding something.

'Right, you'll have to have a go. Maybe I did something wrong. Come with me.'

Before Peter had a chance to reply, the old man had turned and was creeping, shoulders hunched forward, along the side of the building, under the window of one room, then disappearing around the corner once more. Peter took one look at the Covids, then rushed to follow him.

This shorter side of the building was featureless brick and by the time they turned the next corner, Peter had caught up to the large man. He was surprised at the size of the back garden. It was almost twice as wide as their own plot, and although, like their house, it was bordered by the field at the bottom, it seemed longer. Where the lawn fell away to the field was a large mature oak tree, the bottom branches of which hung low enough to block out parts of the horizon. It was a garden his father would have envied.

'Look here, boy,' the old man was pointing to a white plastic casing low down on the brickwork of the house. Major Singh flipped the covering outward, revealing a solid grey box, in a recess of which was the switch. It was pointing to 'On'. Peter bent forward to concentrate as the old man began to explain. 'I want you to start counting, then on the stroke of 30, I want you to push this switch up and then shout as loudly as you can, 'Off'. That will turn the electricity off. Then we'll see what happens.'

'OK.'

'But remember, give me thirty seconds before you do it. I want to get around to the front and see if it works.'

'I understand.'

'Start counting.'

'Yes, one, two, three…'

'Good boy,' said the old man, smiling broadly at Peter before retracing his steps.

Peter's tension grew as he counted, and by the time he reached the end of the count he could no longer be sure that the finger which lay poised on the thick switch even belonged to him. It had slid away, become a separate thing. Twenty-eight...twenty-nine...thirty...It was only when he saw the appendage stub at the switch that he recovered. The switch shifted upwards with a satisfying solidity, but it still took a few further moments before he could remember the other part of the old man's instructions. 'Off!' he bawled as loudly as he could, his voice taking him by surprise in the lazy afternoon silence.

Almost at the same time, he heard a metallic clatter, like a pile of tin cans and glass bottles falling to the ground. The sound came from the front and repeated several times. Then he heard a cry from the old man, urging Peter to join him. Even before he reached the front of the building, Peter could see the eruption of the Covids into the sky, squawking and taking off in every direction.

'Look, Peter-Sir, it's worked!' cried Major Singh. His face was flushed and breathless, fresh perspiration beaded his forehead, leaving the edges of the tight material darkened with sweat.

'What was that noise?' asked Peter.

'That was just the noise of the electricity going off. But look, Peter-Sir, there they go! We've beaten them. We've defeated the Covids!'

Peter was too giddy with excitement to say more, and just stood beside the major, watching as the birds noisily wheeled away from the line, away from the building, startled and aimless.

As the major continued staring at the agitated birds, Peter looked away. The disused fence which had provided their shield lay at a different angle than before and, as he looked closer, to where the panel rested upon the bright silver of the burner, Peter saw that the funnelled lid no longer sat flush to the main body of the burner, but instead lay slightly askew, as though it had been knocked, or shifted.

Peter looked up again and watched as the Covids swung around in lazy circles, heaving out their awkward sound, but not departing.

Instead, they began to circle in ever tighter formations, settling down slowly through the air. The major, too, was looking on in silence.

'Come, Peter-Sir, let's get back behind the screen again, just in case.'

It didn't take long before the crows had settled once again upon the thick wire, croaking and looking malignantly at the pair of humans observing in dismay behind the panel.

'It didn't work,' Peter muttered. 'They've come back.' He couldn't pull his eyes away from the row of Covids. They appeared more potent than ever.

'Don't worry, Peter-Sir, I'll think of something else,' said Major Singh, clambering to his feet once more. 'Better go and turn on the electricity now, otherwise I'll be hungry later.'

Peter was close to tears, and it was only when he heard the major's gentle voice close to him did he realise how much he had succumbed to disappointment.

'Come, child, your mother will be worried about you. I'll walk you to the road, the Covids won't dare attack with both of us here.'

'Yes,' said Peter.

They walked slowly back along the driveway, the only sound the dry crunch of their feet on the stones. Peter was surprised when they reached the tarmac. He had barely thought of the Covids at all, even though they were still on the line and so close now that Peter could make out their claws upon the wire. He was even more surprised to realise that all the way across the stones, the major had settled an arm around his shoulders.

'Cheer up, Peter-Sir. Whoever heard of a war with just one battle?' The major smiled at his joke and looked down at Peter. 'Can you come back tomorrow?'

'Yes, I think so.'

'Good, because I have another idea!'

'You do?'

'I do, but that's enough warfare for one day. Ride home quickly now, Peter-Sir, the Covids might not be still for long.'

With a final furtive glance above him, Peter pushed down hard on the pedals and set off home.

Chapter 11

Peter was in bed when his father returned that evening. His room was not completely dark and he listened in the half-light to the low murmurings of his parents, muted and indistinct from below. The voices came through like the utterings of business associates, and Peter wondered if this was more ominous than the raised voices he often heard.

And then his father came to see him. Peter heard the creaking of the stairs, then the catch and slow open of the door, careful footsteps across the room, followed by the light kiss and waft of outside world that his father drew with him. The kiss was not devoid of tenderness, and for one moment Peter thought about halting his pretence at sleep. But that would bring its own complications, and Peter wasn't sure he had the words to explain how he felt, or how he would even go about beginning to ask his father to save a little of that kindness for someone else.

His father was gone the following morning when Peter arrived in the kitchen. His mother sat at the head of the table, teacup pursed to her lips, but there was little will to drink. Her eyes flickered towards Peter as he closed the door behind him, a reaction to movement rather than anything deliberate, and she remained silent.

'Hello, Mum.'

'Hello, darling.'

'Where's Dad?' It was a stupid thing to say.

'Your father had to leave early for work. He says he'll be back in good time tonight.' She tried to smile but it faded before it had even got going.

Peter went to his mother, wrapped her as much as he could in his arms, squeezing and applying his lips to her cheek. He sucked in the steam from the tea and her morning warmth, and thought he felt her swell as he released her, her hand coming around and sweeping through his hair. He felt he had done something good.

For the next few minutes, and while he ate the cereal and toast his mother had risen to prepare for him, he remained in silence, partly for his mother, partly to listen to the news from the radio. It soon became clear that their actions the previous day had counted for very little; the Covids were continuing, and their campaign appeared to be gathering force, with more deaths, more people in hospital and, most concerning of all, the country's leader was in a hapless state. What would they do if he was to die? Would it be the beginning of the end for them all, leaderless, without direction? But Major Singh was sure of what to do, and not for a moment did Peter doubt him.

When he did speak, to ask permission for another day of outdoor pursuits, he wasn't surprised that his mother accepted. He was quick to perform everything in the house that was expected of him and was soon outside. It was another day direct from the heavens and the sun was already high and strong as he made his way to the shed to collect his bike. As he came to the end of the side passage beside the house, he paused, looking up towards the corkscrew turns of the black wire, checking for Covids. But the wire, like the air, was clear and he was soon feeling the wind breaking before him as he cycled the short distance to the major's house.

'Good morning, little warrior.' Major Singh sprang up from immediately behind the privet hedge, rising like some ancient sea god and surprising Peter even before he had come to a stop. His gloves were mottled with dry mud and in one hand he held some limp weeds. He seemed to be expecting Peter, and his eyes shone, reminding Peter of the polished jet he had seen on a school trip to the coast. They were eyes which spoke of mischief and intent.

'Seen any Covids yet?' he asked.

'No, but I've been looking. And I know they've been killing more people than ever.'

'So I've heard, too. We must stop them. Are you ready to renew the war?'

'Yes, Major Singh!'

'Good boy, Peter-Sir, that's how I like my soldiers, keen and ready.'

Peter glowed in the strange man's praise and the pair walked either side of the hedge until they reached the driveway.

'Come, bring your bike around the back, that's where we need to be this morning.'

'Have you got another idea then?'

'I certainly have. I don't know why I didn't think about it earlier.'

'Oh, why?'

'Well, it's obvious, isn't it? We know what the Covids are, don't we?'

'Yes.'

'And we know that we must scare them away from the line. Take away their power, then make sure they never return. Isn't that right?'

'That's what the owl said.'

'Exactly. So we need to give these Covids the fright of their lives.'

'That's right.'

'Me and you know they're Electric Overlords, but for most people, they are just crows and ravens, correct?'

'They're the same thing.'

Major Singh ushered Peter down a concrete path along the left side of the house, towards the back of the property.

'And what, Peter-Sir, do people use to scarce crows away with?'

Peter paused, unsure what the answer could be.

'Oh, come on, Peter-Sir! You're still sleeping, boy! The thing that scares crows away.' The final words the old man spoke deliberately, taking his time with each one, his eyebrows rising in enquiry, and finally Peter understood.

'A scarecrow!' he cried.

'A scarecrow, yes,' repeated Major Singh, taking Peter's bike and laying it against the side wall. 'Righty-ho, follow me, let's see if we've got anything in the garden which we can use. Ever built a scarecrow before?'

'No.'

'Me neither, but it can't be too difficult.'

Peter followed Major Singh along the path at the rear of the property, until they reached the corner where Peter had turned off the electricity.

'Seen anything so far?'

'No, what am I supposed to be looking for?'

'Anything lying around the garden that could be useful for making a scarecrow with.'

'Oh.'

'Come on, let's have a look in these flower beds.'

Major Singh led them across a section of lawn, the grass already thick with new growth, until they reached some flower beds which ran in curved contours most of the length of the far side of the garden. The first of the year's bloom were appearing, shades of mauve and pink amidst the shiny greenness of fresh leaves. The old man walked slowly, his face absorbing the energy of the spring growth and Peter walked at his side, half noticing the old man, half intent on spying the things they could use for the scarecrow. Shortly before the end of the garden, the deep flowerbeds gave way to a slabbed patio of concentric circles, on top of which was a small table of wrought iron, its mosaic surface of pastel colours faded by long exposure. Two matching chairs stood to either side, and enclosing it all was a weeping birch, its branches hanging like the tentacles of a jelly fish. It reminded Peter of his den.

'Have a good look around here,' said Major Singh, leaning both hands on the edge of the table.

The two sticks were easy to see, protruding into the paving from the flower beds and Peter was quick to pick on them, seizing one with his hands, and holding it to his side, like a guardsman standing to attention.

'What about this?' he cried excitedly.

'Why, that's perfect, Peter-Sir. Well spotted.'

Both sticks were stout, about the width of Peter's wrist, and the longer of the two just pipped his head.

'We'll have to tie them together and make a cross with them. I think I've got some twine in the shed. Then we use some old clothes to put on the sticks, to make it look more realistic. But let's see what else we can find,' said Major Singh.

From the trailing birch, they came to the bottom of the garden. Peter could see that, like his own house, the ground dropped away, and in the no-man's land before the field was a mixture of grasses, wild flowers and stinging nettles. A large comfrey bush, halfway along, had been carefully trimmed around. They walked along the edge of the lawn, and Peter thought how he would defend this larger frontier against advancing hordes from the field. As they passed under the large oak tree, Peter felt the coolness and heightened mystery of the shade. The lower branches, he thought, would be fun to climb into. On the far side of the garden were a series of long, raised vegetable beds, hemmed in by rough wooden boards. Inside the beds, small flexible plastic markers stood improbably white against the peaty soil, alongside each marker a wispy green straggle was beginning to emerge. But Major Singh was pointing towards the field.

'What about that, Peter-Sir?'

It took Peter a few moments to understand what the major was referring to. On top of a large scorched area at the edge of the field was a recently cut bundle of long grasses and scrub weed.

'I was going to burn it,' explained Major Singh. 'But maybe it could come in useful. What do you think, Peter-Sir?'

'Yes! We could use it to put inside the clothes. To make it look larger. To puff it up!'

'Brilliant idea, Peter-Sir. Just brilliant,' said Major Singh. 'Go and pick up a handful, and we can get some more later.'

Peter edged down the side of the garden and cupped an armful of the cut grasses. He was delighted at his contribution.

'You go first, Peter-Sir,' said Major Singh, indicating with a nod of his head the route back up the garden, and keeping a few paces behind the boy. 'Keep an eye open to anything we might be able to use.'

The pair hadn't gone far before Peter shouted out again.

'What about this, Major Singh?'

'What is it, Peter-Sir?'

'Is this any good?'

In his excitement, Peter had dropped the bundle of grasses on the ground and picked up a medium sized grey burlap bag. He held it with one hand to show to Major Singh. Several particles of yellowy dry dirt trickled from the surface of the bag onto the ground next to the raised vegetable patch.

'It was just lying here, on the side of wood.'

'Really?'

'Yes,' replied Peter-Sir. 'This could be his head.'

'His head, you reckon?'

'Yes.'

'It's about the right size. But where are his eyes, nose and mouth?'

'We…we…we could paint, or draw them on!' exclaimed Peter.

'Why yes, of course we could, Peter-Sir. What a good idea. I hadn't thought of that.' The Major's voice was deep and flat and betrayed no emotion.

Peter gave the bag to Major Singh and picked up the grasses. The loose strands tickled his nose as the pair walked back up the garden, towards the grey slatted shed which they reached via a series of stepping stones set into the lawn.

'Leave the grass over there,' said Major Singh, indicating towards where the path ran around the house. 'Then we'll have a look in the shed to see if we can find anything.'

Peter ran to the corner of the house, opening his arms wide and releasing the grasses before turning around and quickly returning to the shed. As he approached, Major Singh was opening the door, the padlock in one hand.

'It's a bit dark in there, but have a look first and see if you can find anything. I'm just going back inside the house to get some scissors to cut the twine.'

When the major returned, Peter was waiting at the door of the shed, a plastic supermarket bag held up triumphantly.

'Look what I found, Major Singh!' Peter was almost singing.

'What is it, Peter-Sir?'

'It's a bag of clothes. Look, here's a shirt, T-shirt, trousers, socks...'

'How did that...oh, never mind. That's perfect.'

'Yes, we can use them to dress the scarecrow with,' Peter said breathlessly.

'Well done, Peter-Sir, you're a first rate scavenger. I bet you could take care of yourself behind enemy lines, eh? Right, take those over there and we'll make a start. I'll just see if I can find the twine.'

The old man was quick to emerge from the shed with a roll of coarse twine and joined Peter who was already sitting on the path next to the house, surrounded by the items he had located around the garden.

The pair worked quietly under the warming sun, but that suited Peter who was happy to watch as Major Singh twisted the twine around the intersection of the two lengths of wood, his hands slow, but precise and strong, and when he pulled the twine taut, the cross section snapped together with a juddering firmness that made Peter jump.

After that, they put the shirt on. It was old, with large black squares thick against a red background. Peter suspected it must have once belonged to Major Singh. Then Peter set to, greedily stuffing the arms and chest with the straw and grass he had carried across. When he ran out, he sprinted to the bottom of the garden to collect more. A pair of worn jeans, stained around the thighs with what might have been dried glue, were hung by twine suspenders over the top branch, hanging down below the putative man's waistline, and Peter repeated the stuffing process, filling the trousers to the brim before hitching them up to meet the shirt.

'Do you want to paint the head, Peter-Sir?' Major Singh held out a black marker pen to the young boy. Peter laid the burlap bag on the stone flagging of the path and began to work on the creature's features. It was fun, but he hesitated when he came to drawing the mouth, unsure whether to give it a goofy grin, or whether a sterner, more sour look would be more appropriate to seeing off the Covids.

After adding some caterpillar eyebrows, Peter declared the head complete, and Major Singh stepped forward with a handful more hay and quickly stuffed the burlap bag, tying it off with twine before using both hands to slot it down onto the exposed end of the wooden cross, like a coronation crowning. Both man and boy stepped back to look at their creation.

'Shall we give him a turban, Peter-Sir?'

'A turban? What's that?'

'One of these,' said Major Singh, leaning forwards to show the boy his head.

'Oh.'

'I don't mind if you don't want to. But he may be the first Sikh scarecrow in the world if he did have one.' Major Singh smiled.

'What's a Sikh, Major Singh?'

'A Sikh, little one, is someone like me, someone who wears a turban, and follows the Sikh religion.'

'Do you have to wear one?'

'If I want to stop all my hair from falling in my eyes, yes. A Sikh, you see, never cuts his hair, or isn't supposed to.'

'Never?'

'Never.' The major spoke so solemnly that Peter waited for the old man to continue. 'It is one of the tenets of our religion. It shows our gratitude to God and distinguishes us from other people. It also means we can recognise others who follow our faith.'

'Have you worn a turban since you were my age?'

'Well, not quite, little one.' The old man turned away, squinting as he looked across the fields, to where the sun spread thickly across the southern sky. His leathery brown skin both reflected and absorbed the light. 'I didn't wear a turban when I first came to England, and I certainly didn't have one when I met Rosie. I'm not sure how she would have reacted had she met me with beard and turban.'

'Who's Rosie?'

'That's a good question, Peter-Sir, and I wish I had a simple answer.' The old man paused, filling with quiet memory. 'But suffice to say that for me she was the loveliest, kindest, most interesting woman I ever met.'

Peter was quiet, waiting.

'Let's leave him as he is, Peter-Sir. I don't want to frighten poor Mrs Proudfoot by having two crazy Sikhs on New Cuttings Lane!'

Peter watched as the major picked up the scarecrow from behind and walked along the back of the house with it. He looked like a Roman standard bearer marching into battle. They slowed when they approached the front of the house, the major drawing closer to the side wall, silently urging Peter to do the same. Then he turned and lowered his voice.

'We need to wait for some Covids to appear, Peter-Sir.'

'OK.'

'Then, to make it work, we need to make them think that the scarecrow is real. We must run behind it and shout out as loudly as we can. Then we'll wait and see what happens.'

From their position at the corner of the house, Peter could see across the front lawn to the stretch of wire. Several Covids were already resting on the line, looking away. Peter nudged the major in the side.

'Shall we do it now?' Peter hissed.

'Negative. Let's wait a little. The more Covids we can scare from the line, the more effective our message will be.'

But they didn't have to wait long. More creatures were appearing all the time, loitering on the wire before occasionally falling away, letting themselves drop to the ground where something was attracting their attention. Soon there were around a dozen of them, spread along the wire, like musical notes on a stave.

'Righty-ho, Peter-Sir. It's now or never. You take one leg, I'll take the other. Make as much noise as you can. Are you ready?'

'Yes, Major Singh!' said Peter, who had already taken hold of the bottom hem of one leg.

'Ready, go!' cried Major Singh.

Man and boy broke cover from the corner of the whitewashed building, running across the lawn, Major Singh holding the central shaft of the scarecrow in his left hand, one flapping trouser leg in the other. As they emerged, Peter heard the roar that came from the old man's throat, something deep and primeval, a battle cry for the ages.

The creatures turned without alarm to look, considering the advancing vision of scarecrow, man and boy, before rising from the line with a heavy, slow beat of their powerful wings, splintering away without coordination. By the time the puffing and panting pair had reached the privet hedge not a single Covid remained on the line.

'It worked, Major Singh!'

'Yes,' replied the major, dropping the scarecrow clumsily against the hedge, gathering himself. 'I think we've done it, Peter-Sir. Did you see the fear in their eyes?'

Peter just beamed. He had been too busy hollering and running to take in much else, but was delighted to know that the Overlords had taken fright.

'Well done, Peter-Sir. Mission accomplished, my little warrior. But we still need to be on our guard that they don't return. It's unlikely, but we must be sure.'

'Yes, Major Singh.'

'So, you go home now and keep watch. If the Covids do come back, we will have to consider carefully our next move. We can't afford to fail another time.'

But Peter had no such doubts about their enemies. Their fright had been extreme, they had scattered to the four winds, disappeared, and even now Peter could imagine the urgent conversations ricocheting along the Covid highway: the Electric Overlords had met their match, could no longer depend on the electricity lines for their power, not when Major Singh and his strike force were around.

The conviction grew in strength as he gathered his cycle, riding under the wire where Major Singh still stood guard with the scarecrow, and not a Covid to be seen in the picture postcard sky. Slowly, over coming days, the world would wake from the darkness and death of the Covid chill, and Peter wondered what words he would use to explain to the assembled media how he and Major Singh had managed it.

It was only as the stones sizzled beneath the tyres as he reached the driveway of home that the first crack in that future came, appearing as a shape, dark and undefined in the west, moving unhurriedly across the sky. It was impossible be more precise at that distance. The stones brought the bike to a halt and Peter peered across the low hedge which separated their house from the neighbour, straining for more clues.

And then he saw the rest of them. Forty, fifty, perhaps more. It didn't matter. They were still a long way off, but flying low and purposefully along the line of the Fassingham road at the bottom of their street. His hands lay rigid on the handlebars as he considered them. Maybe they were fleeing, scattering still from the pummelling they had taken earlier. But there was little fear in their steady progression across the western sky, only definition and resolve.

On an impulse for immediate safety, Peter looked up, directly above him. But the line, thick and potent just metres above his head, was still bare. But it was little relief. A dreadful premonition had already clutched at something deep within him. A question he dared not ask, an answer he knew without seeing, without returning to the edge of the road, without looking backwards, to where he had cycled from, to the stretch of line around the major's house, the line they had cleared just moments previously.

But he went anyway, laying his bicycle flat on the gravel driveway, dropping it like a veil over the dead, and walking trance-like to the edge of the tarmac. Slow turn of the head and there, in the distance, calm and mocking in the morning air, the Electric Overlords had once again taken their positions, their blackness fusing with the wire. Peter tried to cry, but the tears wouldn't come. Instead, he turned away and walked slowly, defeated, past his cycle, straight to the front door.

Chapter 12

Peter slipped quietly through the doorway, not thinking how unusual this was for him. The front door always had an air of formality about it, like the Queen coming for tea, and he seldom entered the house this way.

But he heard the voices in the kitchen immediately, and some cautionary instinct stilled his hand, resisting the temptation to pull the handle too firmly, and it was only when he'd felt the full resistance of the door in its frame did he slowly let his hand rise and fingers unfurl. The return of the Covids had made him more alert, and he placed one foot very deliberately in front of the other as he approached the kitchen. He recognised his mother, but it was only as he took up his position, a body's width from the door, sinking low onto his haunches, that he realised who the other voice belonged to. Mrs Proudfoot. Another tea visit. She must have made her way down the street when Peter was with Major Singh. She was turned away from him, screening his mother, and only if the visitor turned would they notice him. His mother was subdued still, but Mrs Proudfoot's nasally wheeze was unmistakeable.

'I'm surprised that he has any work on at all,' said Mrs Proudfoot. 'The country has gone into lockdown and all the companies have closed or are closing. He must be the only one still working on that estate.'

'Yes, I'm not sure what he does all day long. He tells me he still has jobs on, but I really don't know.'

'Well, I suppose it's good that he still has work to go to. My cousin Teddy has already lost her job. Still, it can't be easy paying the mortgage on a property like this?'

'It's not. We were struggling to pay when the company was fully staffed. But now he's alone, he's not doing anywhere near the same volume of business.'

'Oh, dear,' said Mrs Proudfoot. There was a hint of relish in her reaction. 'Life can be so cruel sometimes, and men so insensitive.'

'What do you mean?'

'Only that it seems to me that men only consider the things that they are interested in. They struggle to care about others. Don't you think, dear?'

'It's only recently he's been like this,' his mother said sadly. 'He was lovely at the start, when we lived in town together.'

'They always are,' Mrs Proudfoot said abruptly, and in the silence that followed Peter could hear the ticking of the kitchen clock. He was being careful with his breathing, taking in slow, lengthy streams of air, and letting them out as calmly as possible. 'Of course,' Mrs Proudfoot continued, 'having never been married myself, I'm not an expert on men, but what I do know is that they tire quickly of routine. They are always on the lookout for novelty. Some people say that men think only from their waist down. I'm sure that's not true for Steve,' she said hurriedly. 'He seems like a lovely man, at least the few times I've met him, but they do say that men have only one thing on their minds. Anyway, at the very least, he should take care of you. Not spend so much time at work, especially in the evenings. Did he ever tell you why he was working late?'

'No, not really.'

'Hmm, and I suppose it would be difficult to check as well?'

'Yes.'

Peter noticed his mother's reluctance to talk, in contrast to the gusto Mrs Proudfoot embraced every phrase with. He wondered how much longer they would be. With his legs tucked tightly beneath him, he could feel the tension in his knees. He would need to move soon. But Mrs Proudfoot was speaking once more.

'But I know how you feel. And it can't be easy for you, with the baby, and that boy doing anything he wants, and breaking the lockdown rules, too.'

'What, Peter?'

'Yes, speaking with Mr Singh.'

'Mr Singh? The man who lives in the end house?'

'Surely the boy has told you all about it?'

'No.'

'But those two have been as thick as thieves over the last few days. He must have mentioned something?'

'Not a thing. I thought he was messing around at the bottom of the garden, in his den.'

'Well, he might have been for some of the time. But I've also been seeing an awful lot of him up at our end of the street recently. A nice boy, but maybe a little irresponsible. I would have thought Mr Singh should have known better, but he just hasn't been the same since Rosie died.'

'Rosie?'

'His wife.' Mrs Proudfoot waited for a further question and when it wasn't forthcoming, she continued. 'She died over a year ago now. Cancer, it was. Just like her sister. She just faded away over a number of months. Mr Singh just hasn't been the same since.'

'In what way?' Peter heard the familiar trace of alarm.

'He just doesn't come out much anymore, and looks so morbid, depressed even. And when I do speak to him, he does say the strangest things. Of course, he's not English, that might be why. They do things differently over there.'

'He's always seemed quite normal to me.'

'But you don't know him as well as I do, do you?'

'He always says 'hello' when I've come across him on the road.'

'Nothing else?'

'No.'

'Ah.'

Peter let his back slide further down the wall, feeling the relief on his straining knees as his bottom made contact with the parquet of the hallway. All he needed to do now to be completely comfortable was stretch his legs out. Beyond the door, Peter could feel his mother's lack of enthusiasm for the conversation. It was like an interview with a medical professional. But Mrs Proudfoot wasn't finished.

'Of course, I wouldn't have mentioned it, but he's not from this country, is he? They have strange customs over there, and even old men have certain urges, don't they?'

'Right.'

'But I'm sure it's nothing.'

'Yes.'

'But I wouldn't have felt right without mentioning it. You can't be too careful, can you?'

Peter's mother didn't reply and Peter decided that it was the right moment to complete his move to a more relaxed position. Then he would stay a little longer, eavesdropping into this adult world, before slipping away silently to his bedroom, a slither up the stairs. First, he stretched his left leg, enjoying the relief of relaxing muscles. But as he moved his right, the ball of twine that they'd used to tie the scarecrow loosened, falling from his pocket to the parquet floor with a dull thud. At any other time it would be easily ignored, but in the silence of the kitchen, the sound was an anomaly, an intrusion.

'Peter, is that you love?'

His mind fizzed with options but in an instant he had made his decision. He would have to feign recent arrival.

'Hello, Mum,' he cried airily, quickly rising, pushing the glass panels and entering the room as casually as he dared. He hoped his easy going show would dissolve any suspicion. But one look at his mum, seated in her normal chair at the end of the table, told him that he had not been successful. She glared at him.

'Why didn't you come in the back way, Peter?'

'I..I was around the front of the house, Mum. I just wanted to go to the toilet.'

'I see,' said his mum. She saw everything, Peter realised. But now was not the time for confession, that would come later, when the guest had departed.

Mrs Proudfoot twisted around uncomfortably in her chair. She wore a smile of smug satisfaction. 'Hello, Peter. I've been seeing a lot of you recently.'

Peter didn't even attempt to reply, and his smile wilted under her steady, probing grimace, examining him for some further reaction and waiting for fresh betrayals.

'I'm going to go upstairs, Mum, OK?'

'Please stay in your room, Peter. I'll be up shortly.'

Peter attempted another smile, turned and trudged upstairs to await the reckoning that all three knew was in store.

*

'Peter, I know it's difficult for you, not seeing your friends, not going to school, but you're not allowed to be close to other people. You can say hello to Mr Singh when you're riding past, but you mustn't go too near him. He could have covid.'

His mother stood with folded arms by the side of his bed, looking down on him. It hadn't taken her long after the visitor left for her to come to see him.

'But Mum, Major Singh and I are trying to get rid of the Covids!'

His mum looked puzzled.

'I don't care Peter, he could still be infectious.'

'You speak to Mrs Proudfoot,' Peter said defiantly.

'That's different. Mrs Proudfoot hasn't left her house. She hasn't been in contact with anybody. Her food is brought in for her.'

'How do you know?'

'She's told me, Peter.'

Peter wondered if his mother was surprised at his belligerence, a feeling which had only grown in the time he spent alone in his room, waiting for his mother to arrive. He couldn't understand why he wasn't allowed to speak with Mr Singh but Mrs Proudfoot was allowed to visit. They weren't even trying to save the world. It was a consideration his mother needed to be reminded of.

'Mr Singh is helping me defeat the Covids, Mum!'

'Peter, please don't start on that again. I know you're trying your best, but it's all a very strange situation, and you're not helping matters by gallivanting around. I've got a good mind to tell your father about this.'

'Please don't, Mum.'

'I just don't want you speaking alone to that man again. Do you understand me?'

'Yes, Mum.'

'Thank you, Peter.'

His mum seemed relieved to have finished with him, and it was only as she carefully drew the door closed behind her did Peter realise that his mother's mind was elsewhere, far beyond a boy's childish foibles. The ticking off had been the act of a dutiful parent, nothing more.

Peter rose briefly and looked from his bedroom window over the lawn and beyond that to the fields which stretched into the distance. Then he lay back on his bed, reliving the morning's events. He kept returning to Mrs Proudfoot's grandmother face, and the look she had given him. It was a look of victory, as though she knew that their latest machinations against the Covids had met with failure. It was the pitying look of an adversary too aware of an uneven battle, an enemy smug in the knowledge of their own superiority.

And then it struck him. It was obvious. Mrs Proudfoot hadn't come to their house to seek solace or friendship with his mother, nor for the tea. Mrs Proudfoot had only one thing on her mind when she had appeared at their house. Because Mrs Proudfoot, Peter now clearly saw, was a Covid spy.

It was the only explanation. That was why she hadn't been attacked by the Covids yet, his mother was sure about that. It also explained why the Covids collected on the line near her house, they were simply awaiting, or giving, orders of some kind. The Electric Overlords had been planning this takeover for many, many years, through generations of men and women. It was only natural that they had a vast underground army of sleeper cells throughout the human population, their eyes and ears into the world of mankind.

Wasn't this how they had managed to penetrate directly into the Prime Minister's house? A Covid spy at the heart of Number 10 Downing Street itself.

Mrs Proudfoot couldn't help but see Peter with Mr Singh, maybe she had overheard them, or the explosion when the electricity was turned off. It would have been easy for her to witness their scarecrow caper that very morning, then receive immediate orders from the Overlords to pay the boy a visit, to scare Peter with the knowledge that he had been rumbled, nothing too obvious, just play with the child a little. Maybe also drop a hint to the boy's mother, neuter him. If the Covids couldn't get to him inside a building, then they would make sure he could no longer get out, let the family do the dirty work for them, divide and rule. It seemed so obvious now.

But as Peter gauged how he could best respond to this new threat, another, far more sinister thought came to him, a version of events he struggled with and didn't want to believe. It was a version in which no-one could be trusted, and which located two elderly humans at one end of the street, a location long favoured by the Covids. The story would see one of those humans playing a role of deliberate meanness, while the other was reserved for a protector and friend. But at the end of the day, when Peter was far away in his own home, lying tired and asleep in bed, these two actors would come together, comparing notes and events of the day, and planning their next moves. They would receive orders from their masters, the Electric Overlords, about how best to deal with the brave few, those like Peter, who were wise to the overall plan. It was a version in which Major Singh was not the kind, avuncular human Peter thought him to be, but was an elaborate double agent, an insider's insider, a Covid spy.

Chapter 13

Deer mayjaw Sing,

Sorry, I canot come and see you. My mum has sed I musent speek to you becoz you mait have Corvid (but I told her you hadent been atakt by them jet). But I want to speek to you. The Corvids are stil here, I saw them on yor line. I stil need yor help to deefeet them. Plees, plees right bac...

Peter

Oh, I forgot, Mrs proudfuut is waching us. I think she is a Corvid spi

Peter tore the sheet of lined paper from the pad that had arrived at the bottom of his Christmas stocking and held it aloft. Some things didn't look quite right, but it would have to do. All the essentials were there, he was sure. Double agent or not, Peter still needed Major Singh. The Electric Overlords were stronger than ever and Peter was despairing at ever getting rid of them. He was running out of options.

Peter wished there was an easy way to get the letter to Major Singh, but with his mother's heightened suspicions, Mrs Proudfoot on the prowl and the Covids anything but cowed, any option was fraught with danger. He would have to be bold, take some risks. He had been forbidden to speak to Mr Singh, but no-one had said anything about his bicycle. That was not out of bounds. He was still free to cycle up and down the lane.

And so it was that a short while after he had completed the letter, and still early enough in the morning to see goose pimples rise on his bare arms, Peter found himself at the front of Major Singh's driveway, leaning across his handlebars, ruminating over what he was about to do. He looked down again towards his hand. The medium sized stone he had found along the track still had grains of dirt on it, some of which had already rubbed off onto the lined paper below it. But that couldn't be helped, collateral damage. The major would still be able to read it.

With a final look around he moved, letting the cycle drop with one hand and sprinting towards the major's house, stones popping under his shoes like camera shutters at a gala dinner. He placed the stone and note clumsily on the doorstep, pressed the doorbell, turned and ran, not daring to look back. It was all over in a matter of seconds, and as he dragged his bike up, still breathing heavily, he wished he had taken more care with placing the paper under the stone. It could very easily fly away if the major didn't come immediately.

Only when he had almost lost sight of the front door did he dare to turn, looking over the low privet hedge to see if anything had happened. But the letter remained on the doorstep, and Peter cycled the rest of the way home, relieved that the letter had been delivered, but uneasy about what would happen to it, unsure, too, whether Mrs Proudfoot had latched on to his fleeting delivery.

He made sure his mum saw him when he returned, waving at her vigorously through the kitchen window, assuring her that he was behaving himself. Then he made his way slowly down the garden, sitting cross legged outside the den on the warm grass. The blackbird would know what he should do next. After all, she had told him about the Electric Overlords in the first place, maybe she could offer some useful intelligence about their strength and intentions at this moment. He might even mention his doubts about Major Singh.

But as he sat on the warm grass, the hedge remained silent, and Peter began to wonder if she had moved, frightened away by the Covids, or worse, silenced forever by them. One less ally. One less friend. Despite the beauty of the day, everything was eerily still, as though someone, or something, had sucked out all sound and movement, pausing and turning off the world. The longer Peter waited, the more ominous and threatening the surroundings became. It was a force which soon brought him to his feet and hurried him back across the lawn, not looking behind even as the back door closed after him.

Once inside, he was relieved to hear the radio and his mother's sing along voice, and from the cot next to the table, Julia, too, was making her contributions. Feeling safer inside, Peter was content to flit between the kitchen and his bedroom for what remained of the morning.

'Are you going out this afternoon, love?' his mother asked as she removed his empty plate from in front of him after lunch.

'I don't know, Mum,' he replied. 'I might just stay indoors. It's too warm outside.'

'Too warm!' she scoffed. 'It's lovely out there, Peter. I'm going to walk down the road with Julia after this. Come with us.'

Peter wasn't sure if this was a request or order, so just smiled at his mother. But his inactivity was troubling him. A walk with the family would be a distraction, an antidote to the unresolved chaos of the Covids.

'Ok, Mum,' Peter said, rising from the table and readying himself.

A short time later, they were all on the tarmac, in front of the house. They walked slowly together beside the open pram from where his sister lay on her back, all giggles and writhing limbs in the sparkling sunlight. At first Peter found himself looking nervously up towards the thick wrappings of the electricity line which they followed down the narrow road. But there were no dark Covids to be seen, and Peter soon stopped looking, instead following his mother's suggestions of curious items in the front gardens of the houses they passed; a disused telephone box in one, a cockerel weather vane another, pointing down to fading daffodils by the side of the road, up to the Spring blossom of cherry and apple trees and, from far away, the sound of a pheasant shrieking. As he responded, Peter thought he saw glimpses of the child in his mother, the reflecting sun lifting her whole face into happiness and joy.

When they reached the main road, they turned towards Fassingham, walking along until there were no more houses. A little beyond, the pavement stopped abruptly, and the pair turned and made their way back, chatting about nothing and everything. Peter almost forgot he was in the middle of a war.

They were about halfway up their lane when Peter lifted his head and saw the figure walking towards them. His heart skipped a beat. There could be no doubt. The erect bearing, slow but deliberate walk, and turban which arched skyward like some celestial pointer. Mr Singh. Like seeing an old acquaintance in a novel setting, Peter found himself confused. What was Mr Singh doing walking here? Why wasn't he at home? Only as the distance between them receded did Peter start making sense of the situation; that Mr Singh lived on this street, and that he, too, had a right to walk along it. And with realisation came the questions. Was Mr Singh looking for him or just out for a walk? Had he read Peter's note? Was this his response? Or was Mr Singh fleeing from the Covids?

But Mr Singh didn't look scared. In fact, Mr Singh didn't look anything at all as he approached the pair. It was impossible to read any expression in the weathered face of the old man. Inscrutable. As they drew closer he didn't even look at Peter, his eyes fixed forwards, and it was only when his mother called out a breezy greeting, did the man turn to look across, a flicker of the dark eyes.

'Good afternoon.' The voice was low and formal, a thing of adults. He made no attempt to stop, and even less to engage Peter, who resisted, with some effort, the temptation to turn around and call out at Mr Singh's retreating back. It was as though Peter had never existed.

After a few moments pushing the pram in silence, his mother spoke.

'What did you talk to Mr Singh about, Peter?'

Peter thought quickly.

'Oh, not much, Mum. Just about, er, my bike.'

'Really?'

'Yes, he said he had a similar one when he was younger.'

'Ah.'

Peter wasn't sure if his mother believed him, but he was still reeling from the brief encounter with Mr Singh, his erstwhile ally, who had just completely blanked him. There must be a reason. It was only as they reached the final yards before their driveway that Peter realised why. He rushed forward, beyond his mother, before stopping at the entrance to their driveway and posing uncomfortably with his foot on the same stone that he had laid at Mr Singh's door that very morning. He felt like a footballer posing with a ball beneath his boot. But the stone wasn't large, and if his mother noticed his odd stance, she said nothing, just smiling, still embalmed in the calm the walk had produced within her. When she had disappeared around the front of the building, Peter bent down and recovered what he knew he would find. A piece of paper.

Dear Peter-Sir,

Thank you for your note.

The Covids (Electric Overlords) are indeed getting stronger. I have seen them, too. We must marshal our forces. Time is of the essence.

Come to see me, this afternoon (Wednesday) at 4 p.m. Come the back way, via the field. That will be safer. Watch out for Covids.

Until then.

MS

p.s. I agree we must watch Mrs P carefully.

Peter struggled to mask his excitement as he swung his head around the backdoor of the house and looked up at the clock. There was still an hour to spare.

'Mum, can I carry on playing outside please?' he said as casually as he could manage. But his mother was busy with Julia, who was hungry after the burst of fresh air, and whatever she muttered in reply, Peter took as an agreement of sorts before quickly closing the door and running to the bottom of the garden. There he stopped, looking across the bright green of the spring crop in the field.

The route along the field to Major Singh's house wasn't a long journey, not further than a few hundred yards, but the truth was

Peter had never been beyond the bottom of the garden before. He never had a reason to, but he realised that doing so now would open himself up to the gazes of all those south facing houses. Anyone who happened to be looking from the back windows would easily see him. He wouldn't be on their property, but he would still be an intruder, an unsolicited movement in the landscape. An aberration.

He spent the intervening time turning it over in his mind, occasionally darting back up the garden, making a show of his presence to his mother. By four o clock he was in position and, after a quick glance to check for his mother at the kitchen window he moved, dropping down the slope before moving quickly along the dried rut between gardens and the first furrow of the field. He kept low, not daring to look to his left, praying that no-one would see him and escalate matters to his mother. He had been instructed to keep away from Mr Singh. Now he was doing the exact opposite. Appealing to his mother about saving humanity was not likely to be met with understanding. Peter saw that clearly now.

But no arresting shouts came, and when he reached the far end of the field, Peter was relieved to see Mr Singh leaning over the vegetable beds on the far side of the garden. As he climbed the shallow embankment and made his way onto the grass lawn, Peter called out and the old man turned slowly.

'Ah, little one. You got my note. Well done!' cried Major Singh. There was little trace of the formality of earlier.

'Oh, Major Singh. It's awful,' Peter began hurriedly. 'The Covids haven't gone away. I saw them come straight back to the line outside your house. Then I saw more of them when I got back to mine, and then I heard Mrs Proudfoot talking about you, about us, and…'

'Why don't you slow down, Peter-Sir, and tell me all about it. I'm struggling to keep up with you.'

Mr Singh led Peter over to the birch tree in the corner of the garden, sweeping back the tendrils of the falling branches as he led them inside. It was cooler in the shade and, sitting down on the hard chair, Peter felt calmer, beginning his story again from when he had left Mr Singh the previous day. He didn't mention Mrs Proudfoot's concerns about Mr Singh's character. He wouldn't have known how to.

'So, your mother and Mrs Proudfoot are concerned that I might have Covid, and pass it on to you?' mused Major Singh.

'Yes.'

'And you suspect that Mrs Proudfoot is working with the Overlords to undermine our efforts?'

'I think she knows what we are trying to do.'

'And is trying to stop us?'

'Yes. That's why there are always lots of Covids at this end of the street.'

'Why so?'

'Because she is receiving orders from the Overlords. They're telling her about us, about me,' Peter corrected, startled by the slip of logic he had been unable to avoid, a door opened which he hadn't wanted to. He was unable to meet Major Singh's steady gaze.

'I, too, live at this end of the street, Peter-Sir.'

'Yes, I know Major Singh.'

'Is it not possible that I, too, could be a Covid spy, a double agent for the Overlords?'

'I...I...'

'It is something you have considered, is it not, Peter-Sir?'

'I'm not sure.'

'I would be surprised if a boy as smart as you hadn't thought of such a possibility.'

'I don't really know.'

'But I can see in your hesitation that you have had such thoughts. Both I and Mrs Proudfoot could be in cahoots with the Overlords, part of their effort to take over the earth with this Covid virus. We know that you are the biggest threat to our long held plans for world domination, and that we must join forces to stop you, to crush you, so that no obstacle stands in our way. Is that not so, Peter-Sir?'

The major spoke with an intensity Peter found unsettling. He became aware of his surroundings. Nobody knew where he was, or who he was with. If anything was to happen, who would think to look here? Major Singh's arm was poised on the table, a short distance away from him. Peter knew how strong Major Singh, despite his white beard and wafer skin, still was. Once caught, Peter wouldn't stand a chance.

Then Major Singh looked away, releasing the boy from his gaze and tossing his head to one side.

'Unfortunately, for both of us, there is no way of really knowing, or proving, if I am in league with these beasts or not. Everything I say to you now, all the things we've been doing to rid ourselves of the Overlord threat, could be a sham. You understand what that means, boy? The evidence is not clear, either way. So you have a choice, Peter-Sir. You can either take a leap of faith and choose to believe me, and we will continue our battle. Or not, and you can drift home and not return. It is, like much in life, a question of faith.'

'But the Covids are real, aren't they? That's not a question of faith?'

'Are they, Peter-Sir? Are they real? You have your truth about the Covids, our Government daily gives us its version. But there are many truths, I think. If we were Babylonians we might say that all this was written in the stars, in the Roman world, this disruption might be interpreted as an omen that one of their many Gods was displeased, for a monk of the middle ages, these infections and deaths would be a clear sign from the one true God that people were being punished for their sins. All these people, Peter-Sir, were convinced of their truths. And maybe in the future, hundreds of years from now, people will look on this Covid crisis as neither a thing of science, heavenly omen or message from the Gods, but something we can't even begin to imagine now. Truth, Peter-Sir, is a slippery thing, especially over time. We have certitude in all these things, Peter-Sir, only because we have faith, whether we are aware of that faith, or not.' Major Singh stopped and smiled at Peter.

'Maybe I'm confusing you, Peter-Sir. I'm sorry. I just sometimes like to imagine how things would be if we lived in a different time, that's all.'

'But that's not possible, Major Singh, living at another time.'

'Well, not as myself, of course not. There's only one Major Singh, and he's the old chap sitting next to you now.' Peter watched as Mr Singh raised his eyebrows mockingly. 'But, of course, I could have been around as some other person, or thing, in another life. Who knows, maybe I was even a crow in one of my previous lives. That would be ironic, wouldn't it?'

'What do you mean, previous life, Mr Singh?'

'For us Sikhs, as for many other religions, this body is only my current form. Over time, I have appeared in many different guises. When the body dies, the soul lives on, transforming and returning in a different physical manifestation. Not necessarily as a man, but any creature.'

'Oh.'

'It is all part of the cycle of life.'

'Do you remember what you were before?'

'Unfortunately not. Do you?'

'I don't think so, no,' said Peter, considering. 'And can you choose what you come back as in the future?'

'Well, maybe,' the old man looked away, across the sunlit lawn. 'Maybe if you wish hard enough, then you'll come back as that thing.'

'What would you like to come back as next, Major Singh? A bird?'

'A bird? Perhaps, but definitely not a crow, raven or rook, or any type of Overlord,' Mr Singh smiled before continuing. 'A hawk perhaps, swift and deadly. Or maybe just a simple lark.'

'What's a lark, Major Singh?'

'A lark, Peter-Sir? Oh, there's nothing fancy about larks. They're just average sized, with creamy brown feathers, though some have got a white patch around the throat, like me.' Major Singh tugged playfully at his beard before continuing. 'And their song is quite ordinary compared to other birds, more an insistent chit chat really. But, I've always found it full of joy. They hold nothing back, you see.'

Peter saw the old man raise his head, looking out of the bower. He waited for him to continue.

'Actually, I have a dream about larks, Peter-Sir. I've had it quite a lot recently. Well, I think it's a dream, but it might once have happened. I see Rosie and myself, on a warm summer's day, not unlike today, and we're lying together in long grass in the corner of a field. There's no-one else around and we're on our backs, looking up at the blue sky, watching the clouds drift past, not saying much, just looking and listening. And somewhere up above us, so high that we can hardly see them, are a pair of larks, dancing around each other in the air, and as they dance they are singing, singing their hearts out. It feels like they are singing for all that is good and healthy and free in the world. And it's just me and Rosie, together, in each other's arms.'

Major Singh was perfectly still, his black eyes focussed on the distance, and Peter dared not move. He held his breath, carefully observing the quiet of the old man. Suddenly, Major Singh caught himself, looking smartly towards Peter.

'But enough of that,' he said. 'We've got things to do. We must try again to rid ourselves of the Covids from the line. That is the only way to defeat them.'

'But what if Mrs Proudfoot sees us? She'll tell my mum.'

'Then we'll have to make sure she doesn't see us.'

'How?'

'I have a plan.'

'You do?'

Peter's eyes opened wide. This was more like it.

'Come tomorrow morning, the same way, along the field.'

'Yes, Major Singh!'

Peter jumped from the seat, descended into the field and ran as quickly as he could back home. As he ran he felt the dry wind giving way in front of him. Not once did he think about anyone watching from the formless houses.

Chapter 14

Peter wasted no time in reaching the old Sikh's house the following day. His sister had been unsettled during the night and Peter saw at once when he came down to breakfast that his mother had borne the brunt off it. Her dressing gown was carelessly fastened, revealing too much of her blue pyjamas, and her untied hair fell without form around her sleepy eyes. She shuffled from point to point in the kitchen, and only nodded her agreement when Peter told her of his plans to play outside. Even when she stood at the sink looking towards the den where Peter had deliberately placed himself, he doubted she even saw him.

But he took no chances, staying close to his play shelter, holding a stick as sign of his playful belligerence, waiting for the moment his mother was no longer at the window. When she moved away he reacted, running quickly to the end of the garden, taking the embankment in one leap, and then maintaining momentum as he continued along the side of the field. Today, he was less concerned today about onlookers, more excited about what Major Singh had in store for him.

His anticipation only grew when he jumped onto the major's lawn and saw the old man emerging from the shed. Peter hardly recognised him. Gone were the baggy pastel shades, and in their place was the dark green of combat. On his head, a black turban, wound tightly, and on top of which lay some netting that might once have provided protection from greedy birds. He wore stout leather boots and Peter could see how the laces had been wound with precision around the top of each one.

'Major Singh!' exclaimed Peter.

'Ah, Peter-Sir. And a very good morning to you. Impressed eh?' the old man motioned to his body. 'I thought we'd need it this morning. We've got a very important mission. We can't afford to fail another time.'

'I know, Major Singh.'

'If we want to save the world, we need to strike the Overlords hard, hit them where it hurts.' The old man leant forward and fixed Peter with his stern gaze. 'There can be no mistakes, Peter-Sir.'

'No, Major Singh.'

'And your mother doesn't know you're here?'

'I don't think so.'

Well,' Major Singh seemed a little unsure, 'maybe it's for the best. But if that's the case we can't be long. We'll have to move quickly. Understand?'

'Yes, Major Singh.'

'Righty-ho. Come, let me show you something.'

'What are we doing, Major Singh?'

But the old man didn't answer, instead returning inside the darkness of the shed, only to emerge moments later holding two Y shaped contraptions.

'Ever seen one of these before, little one?'

The major held up one of the instruments and Peter could see where the branches had been recently cut, the tenuous annual growth rings a faint blue against the creamy wood. A rope was attached to two ends. It was the same stretchy cord he had seen his father use occasionally to tie things with. In the middle of the multi-coloured cord, Mr Singh had managed to affix a piece of rubber, part of a bicycle inner tube maybe.

'It's a catapult,' said Mr Singh. 'This time, we can't afford to play games with these monsters. This time, Peter-Sir, we need to kill.'

'Yes, Major Singh.'

'Are you ready to kill, Peter-Sir?' Major Singh was closer now and Peter felt something jerk inside him.

'I think so, Major Singh.'

'Good boy,' said the old man gruffly. 'They're easy to use, all you have to do…'

And for the next few minutes, man and boy took turns with their catapults. Each would take a stone from the lightweight cotton bag Mr Singh had hung from his side, fitting them in to the rubber before aiming high into the sky, pulling back until the cord would stretch no further and then releasing the shot, watching as each projectile arced upwards before landing in the arable field beyond the garden. Occasionally, Major Singh settled behind Peter, holding and instructing him to keep both hands strong and firm. In the still morning air, the scent of the old man was exotic and bold, a smell from an ancient time in a faraway land. It was the smell of pure adventure.

'You're getting the hang of it,' said Major Singh shortly. 'But do you think you can do it when it really counts?'

'I think so, Major Singh.'

'Alright, we'll see, are you ready for battle then?'

'Oh, yes, Major Singh,' Peter cried excitedly, moving away from the major, back up the lawn.

'Where are you off to, boy?' exclaimed the major. 'You're not going like that, are you?'

Peter was confused.

'The Overlords will spot you a mile off with that pasty face,' said the major. 'We need to get close and not be seen. Do you know how we do that?'

'No, Major Singh.'

'Camouflage, boy. That's what we need. Ever worn any camouflage, Peter-Sir?'

'No, Major Singh.'

The old Sikh smiled and told Peter to follow him, back to the shed. Again he disappeared inside, emerging seconds after with an old saucer, inside of which was what looked like a brown sludge.

'Righty-ho, Peter-Sir, here's something I think we can use. Maybe we need just a little mud to finish it off. Pop down to the vegetables and scoop a layer of dirt and bring it back here.'

Once Peter had retrieved the peaty soil and dropped it into the mixture, Major Singh brought out a small penknife and stirred the mixture. It looked like some volcanic pit of earthy lava. Then the pair sat down close to the side of the house, the shallow dish in front of them. Mr Singh dipped two fingers firmly into the mixture.

'I will do you first of all, Peter-Sir, keep your eyes firmly closed, and make a note of where I am putting the mixture.'

Peter closed his eyes and an instant after he felt the major's fingers heavy and firm slide across his cheek. Small lumps of the mud crumbled away, but Peter could feel the paste sticking. From Peter's cheeks, the old man moved upwards, raising the boy's fringe with one hand while applying the cold paste with the other. The major finished off by running both hands under Peter's jowls. Peter thought he had never felt so alive.

'Well, I think that should just about do it,' said the major, leaning back like an artist admiring his work. 'Do you want to see yourself?'

Peter was too excited to wonder where Major Singh had produced the small circular flip mirror from, and it took a few moments for him to keep still enough to appreciate his transformation. In truth, he hardly recognised himself, it was only the hair which looked half familiar, the rest of him had been transformed into a jungle savage or creature from the bush. Peter was speechless.

'Quite a change, eh?' said Major Singh, still holding the small mirror steady in front of the transfixed child. 'Right, now it's your turn.'

At first Peter recoiled when he felt the lumpy paste on his fingers. The thought of touching the old man's leathery skin and defiling the pristine white beard was too much.

'Come now, boy, don't be scared. Slap it on!' the major cried. He was enjoying himself. 'Look, like this.' Major Singh brushed Peter's hand aside, taking a dollop of the paste and smearing it on one side of his beard. It was all the incentive Peter needed and, excited by his own transformation, he proceeded to press layer upon layer onto the old man's skin, stopping only where the folds of the turban wouldn't let him reach any further. Once he had grown used to the stiffness of the old man's bristles, Peter was diligent in his coverage, ensuring that no white remained, encouraged all the time by Major Singh's cries of 'full coverage, boy, full coverage.'

When Peter finally drew away, the major asked if Peter was satisfied.

'Yes, I think so, Major Singh.'

'Very good, boy. Well done. Just one more thing to do. My head.'

The turban was a simple affair. The old man sat stock still as Peter flitted around, like a fussy hairdresser, placing foliage he had retrieved from the garden wherever he could into the netting, hardly noticing the major's descriptions of the need to blend in.

'Enjoying yourself, boy?' the major asked when Peter had almost run out of greenery.

'Sorry, Major Singh, what did you say?' Peter had been concentrating too hard on the foliage.

'Nothing, boy, nothing. Just keep going. You're doing a grand job. We should be able to get up nice and close to the Covids after this.'

When they had finished, the old man and boy picked up the catapults and bag of stones and walked confidently to the side of the house where they had gone previously. As they had done with the scarecrow they slowed as they came close to the front, keeping tighter to the wall and ducking down as they reached the front lawn. Peter, a short pace behind, mimicked the old man. They were like a pair of pantomime thieves.

'Righty-ho, Peter-Sir. This is where it gets interesting,' whispered Major Singh, now crouched by the front wall of the building. A large stretch of the wire was visible across the front of the property, and Peter could see a couple of Covids already positioned on it.

'Do you see that barrier there?' Mr Singh motioned with his eyes to the centre of the lawn where, instead of a neat spread of grass, was what looked like a cross between a bonfire and section of hedge. It was as tall as Peter and wide enough for two people to crouch behind and not be seen. Peter wondered how it had got there, but this wasn't the time to ask. The old man was talking again.

'We have to get there without the Covids seeing us, understand?'

'Yes, Major Singh,' said Peter. He understood nothing.

'Follow me,' urged Major Singh who settled with some difficulty onto the grass and began to crawl on elbows and knees across the lawn, towards the barrier of cut branches and grasses. Peter slid easily onto his front and wriggled forwards, smiling with glee as he passed the old man who, after his initial start, had slowed, each movement more ponderous than the previous, like an old tortoise making his way to pasture. By the time both man and boy were lying behind the makeshift barricade, the old man was breathing heavily and it was a few moments before either spoke.

'Did they see us?' said Peter, keeping his voice low. The electricity line with the Covids on was only half a dozen yards away, and Peter could feel his heart thumping.

'I don't think so.'

'Good. What do we do now?'

'Have a look how many Covids there are on the line,' said Major Singh, beginning to collect himself. 'Keep low down, though. We don't want them seeing us.'

Peter pulled himself to his knees and peeped over the rim of the foliage. He counted quickly before bobbing down again.

'I only saw three, Major Singh.'

'Three, eh?'

'Yes, shall we start firing at them now?'

'Negative, soldier. Let's wait until a few more show up. More of them will make an easier target.'

Major Singh had pulled himself up to a sitting position, but Peter could still see the rise and fall of his chest beneath the army green jumper. For a while they sat quietly, Mr Singh with his back to the structure, occasionally turning to Peter and asking him to check if any more had arrived. Peter felt disappointed at the delay. He was keen to try out his catapult again.

'How long do we have to wait, Major Singh?'

'Patience, little one,' replied the old man.

'But we don't want them to get away.'

'Just a few more minutes.'

Despite his disappointment, Peter kept quiet, happy to be part of the adventure, a faithful lieutenant to the major. He couldn't imagine doing this with his own father. It was the major who broke the long silence, chuckling to himself.

'Ha, this reminds me a little of Longewala.'

'Longewala, what's that?' said Peter.

'It was a battle, many years ago now.'

'Were you there?'

'I was, little one, I was. Just waiting for the Pakistan army to come across. It was night time and we waited many hours. Then we heard their tanks coming through the darkness. A low rumble at first, but then they got closer and closer. We didn't have any tanks of our own and there weren't many of us. That night, we really knew fear.' The old man had slowed and it was only when the silence had stretched longer than he could bear did Peter speak.

'Didn't you have any catapults, Major Singh?'

'Catapults, eh?' the major stirred and looked at Peter in surprise. 'Why no, we didn't Peter-Sir, but I wish we had had. That would have made things easier for us, for sure...' the old man paused, wrinkling his painted nose. 'Anyway, to business, any more of the beasts out there?'

Peter jumped up like a jack in the box.

'Maybe a few more, yes, Major Singh.'

'Righty-ho, time to go then. Can't leave it too late, can we? Remember, stand tall, wrist strong, aim true. Got it?'

'Got it,' said Peter with relish.

'Here we go then, Peter-Sir. Fire at will!'

The two warriors leapt to their feet and began firing at the inert creatures on the line. There the pair stood, Peter bending down regularly to restock with the stones from the bag which the major had left on the ground, Major Singh, pulling the stones from his trouser pocket. The old man's shots rose strong and fast, passing close to the birds every time, extending in a long arc before falling in the fallow land the other side of the road. Peter, more desperate to get each shot away, would often shank his attempt, the projectile dribbling onto the grass lawn in front of the barrier, or landing with a brittle sound as it bounced off the asphalt of the road. Major Singh would chortle and bend to help the boy.

'Try again, little one, keep your front hand steady and strong, that's the way.'

The Covids seemed unperturbed in the face of the attacking force. Occasionally, one would turn and stare for a few moments before rising languidly, unconcerned it seemed by the messy volleys. Peter was having too much fun to really notice.

'Peter-Sir, why don't you pick up some of those stones from the garden so we can use again?' suggested Major Singh when they were running low from the bag. He motioned with his head to the grass between the barrier and the privet hedge. 'I'll keep them at bay.'

Peter rushed forwards, scampering around and picking up the failed shots. Suddenly Major Singh cried out.

'I got one, Peter-Sir! I think I got one!'

'Where? How?' Peter cried, unsure where to look.

'I hit it clean on the breast, I saw it fall, just the other side of the privet hedge, I think, or near the hedge. Have a look.'

As Peter approached the hedge, the Covids took fright, launching into the air. But Peter hardly noticed, so frantically was he scanning around for the fallen creature.

'I can't see anything,' said Peter after a while.

'Me, neither,' replied Major Singh who had emerged from behind the barrier to help with the search. 'Shall we check around the front?'

The pair traced their way along the hedge until they reached the driveway entrance. From there Peter moved quickly, slipping around the corner and onto the road, certain that the dead creature could only be somewhere along the front.

When he saw it, halfway along and just under where the Covids had been perched, he ran forwards, bending down to take a closer look. The creature lay just off the tarmac, amongst the dead twigs and scrub under the hedge.

'It's here, Mr Singh, it's here!'

It was definitely a Covid, but as he examined the creature more closely, Peter was unable to stem a rising sense of disappointment. It was smaller than the creatures on the line, its feathers drab and dusty, and instead of the fiery malevolence that shone from the eye of every live Covid, this creature's stare was glassy and dull. Such a kill was unworthy of their preparation and attention, and Peter wondered if this really would be enough to see off the Covids. It was an easy victory for such a massive problem. Something just wasn't right.

'We did it Peter-Sir,' said Major Singh, coming up behind Peter.

'Yes, Major Singh.'

'Is anything the matter, little one?'

'No, nothing.'

'Righty-ho then, all we have to do now is hang this corpse up somewhere around here, and that will be the final message to these Overlords. They will never dare to return after this brave act.'

Peter stood back and watched as Mr Singh busied himself, bending down to pick up the bird by its tail, and then casting around for somewhere to hang it. The creature looked limp and bedraggled, like a drowning animal pulled to safety. He should be feeling the elation of victory but instead he felt cheated. He was annoyed, too, that even Major Singh had fallen for it. Maybe there really was something to his suspicions about the old man.

Looking away, across the road, Peter could see the top of Mrs Proudfoot's front window. Had she played a part in this pretence? She had already betrayed him to his mother. Was she now trying to humiliate him further with this trick? That would be typical of her. Peter felt a shifting and before he knew it, he had taken one of the stones he had found on the lawn, lodged it into the rubbery compound of the sling and, with the accumulated skill of their earlier practice, let loose straight at the offending window. As he fired, Major Singh turned, catching Peter. Both heard the dry crack as the stone found its mark on the anonymous pane of Mrs Proudfoot's front room. The sound brought Peter round and he wondered how Major Singh would react. The old man looked concerned.

'Peter-Sir,' he began slowly. 'I don't think we should have done that.'

Peter didn't reply. There was nothing to say. With the act now over, the pique of anger had vanished as quickly as it had arisen. He wondered what had possessed him.

'That may have consequences,' said Mr Singh sombrely.

Chapter 15

He wasn't wrong, either. His mother was already on the lawn when he returned, and he paused as he reached the shallow rise to their garden, hunching down low and keenly eyeing his mother further up the garden, by the shed. There was still a chance she hadn't checked his den, and if that was the case, he might still be able to blag it. Indeed, if Mrs Proudfoot hadn't called, or hadn't even noticed the assault on her property, she might not even be looking for him. He didn't want to assume guilt if there was no evidence against him.

With her back turned to him, Peter glided onto the lawn, slowing his pace as he ambled onto the grass, hoping that his easy going saunter might give some protection.

But he had barely made it past the den when his mother turned abruptly and stared straight at him. One look at her face told Peter at once that Mr Singh's prediction had been correct. There would be no escape, and as he trudged slowly towards his mother, like a prisoner to the gallows, he tried hard not to predict what she would say, or how he would respond. It just seemed like extending the agony.

'Peter,' she started sharply, 'this has gone beyond a joke, Mrs Proudfoot has just…'

For the next few minutes, Peter stared mutely at his mother as she ticked off his follies; telling of Mrs Proudfoot's outrage, her own maternal embarrassment, the sanctions he was to suffer, and the searing injunction never to speak to the dangerous Mr Singh again. It was the tone which hurt the most, a voice which slid from exasperation to disappointment and, finally, to quiet despair. Something which came from deeper currents than those caused by an errant boy. But wherever it came from, it reached deep inside him and, almost unawares, he felt the emotion bouncing back, rising hot and watery as the tears pushed slowly from his eyes, dribbling freely down his face.

'But Mum,' he tried to explain, 'we're saving the world from the Electric Overlords. They're on the line outside Mr Singh's house. They're the ones that are killing all these people. Mr Singh says that we can stop all that if we frighten them off. That's what we've been trying to do.'

His mother exhaled deeply. 'Peter, you're only making matters worse. This business about the Covids and the crows is just silly. It's just your imagination, and Mr Singh is not a well man. You can't go firing stones at people's houses. You just can't. Now get back inside and stay there for the rest of the day.'

It was only as Peter limped through the kitchen, into the hallway, that he cared to look up, catching his reflection in the mirror and seeing what his mum must also have immediately seen, his face barely recognisable beneath the thick welts of mud and slime from the camouflage. He could see, too, where the salty lines of his tears had cut channels into the darkness.

*

There was nothing good about the following day, Good Friday. He had been forbidden to leave the house and he felt his mother's extra vigilance on him as something strange and oppressive. He tried playing with his sister on the living room floor, bathing in the warmth of his mother's approval as he played peek-a-boo with the baby who was rolling on the soft carpet. But it was only a temporary diversion, and for much of the day he withdrew to his room where he tried, and failed, to find engagement with the Eye Pad, before moving to his window, leaning on the sill and looking out across the back garden, to his den, and the wide fields beyond.

He wasn't surprised to see the Covids return, but their appearance in the bare branches of the large ash tree, still managed to stun. With each harsh rasp from the creatures, Peter felt his defeat and uselessness even more, the betrayal of the promise he had made to the mother blackbird, and his own crass act with the catapult which had let down Major Singh. Many more people would now die because he had failed to defeat the Covids.

By way of punishment, he slid in to the next room, the spare room that gave out onto the road, and there, upon the thick wire, next to the telegraph pole, were two large Covids, both looking away to the north, but Peter knew the truth. They had been put on guard for him. Craning his neck, Peter looked towards Mr Singh's house, seeking confirmation of the worst, and when he did see them, dense on the line, he was hardly surprised. The Electric Overlords were more numerous than ever. They had won and, despite Mr Singh's help, he had been what he had always been, an eight year old boy trying to take on a conspiracy a million years in the making, taking place at a million different places across the face of the country, the whole world. Who did he think he was?

*

His mother and father quarrelled later that evening. Peter had helped dry the dishes after dinner, before retreating upstairs, whilst below the two voices had become gradually more strained. Peter listened quietly as the two adults, thrown back on their own company, locked wills again.

'Look, Donna, I'll only be out for a few hours.'

'But it's a weekend. Why couldn't you do it during the week?'

'I've told you, Donna, it's urgent. They only let me know yesterday, we finished the print work today and they need it by Monday. It's only local, in Hoveringham, it'll take me a couple of hours at most.'

'Why can't Gary take it? He's looking for work, isn't he?'

'It's not fair to ask him to do it over the weekend. He's got his family to think about.'

'And what about your family?'

'That's not fair, Donna.'

'Isn't it? Look, I'm here all week, looking after these two. It'd be nice to have a break now and again.'

'You don't think I'm doing any work then? Is that it?'

'Steve, I really don't know what you do when you're out.'

'What's that supposed to mean?'

'Whatever you take it to mean.'

'You what?'

But Peter didn't hear his mother's answer. He had risen from his bed and closed the door, half blocking the sound, before slipping the headphone jack into the Eye Pad and completing the silence. He fell asleep with the headphones still wrapped around his head, knowing that tomorrow couldn't come soon enough.

*

By the following morning, the temperature between his parents had cooled, but not disappeared, and Peter couldn't avoid his mother's determined disengagement, pointedly busying herself around the kitchen, giving space for his father's false and slightly forced ebullience, deliberately targeting Peter for conversation.

'Going outside today, Son? Doesn't look quite so nice out there this morning.'

Peter was surprised at the question.

'It depends if I'm allowed, Dad.'

'Allowed?'

'Yes, Dad, after…the other day.'

'Oh, yes, I heard. Your mum's had a word with you about that, hasn't she?'

'Yes, Dad.'

'Good. Well if you are allowed out, then make sure you go nowhere near that old man. Understood?'

'Yes, Dad.'

'He can go out as long as he stays in the garden. No going on his bike,' snapped his mother without looking around from where she was polishing the granite worktop.

'Yes, Son,' his father continued, 'we need to stay at home if we can these days. Over one thousand people died of Covid yesterday, you know?'

'A thousand?'

'Yes, some sort of record for deaths in one day, I think. If we go on at this rate, there won't be any of us left!'

It was difficult to know if his father was joking.

'When do you think it will all end, Dad?'

'Oh, I don't know, Son. I heard someone say that the lockdown was beginning to pay off, but I can't see it. I reckon we'll be like this for another couple of months at least.'

There was a clattering from the end of the kitchen closest to the window where his mother had been cleaning. She had knocked over the salt cellar, hard against the granite worktop, a reaction maybe to her husband's prediction. Peter, too, wondered if he could spend another two months in this way, and watched as his father rose from his chair, coming around the table to rustle his hair and then turning to face his wife.

'I shouldn't be more than a couple of hours, love.'

But his mother didn't respond, her back still towards her husband, her elbow and forearm pumping at the speckled surface like a bursting crankshaft, the only reply a grunt that rose from her diaphragm and filled the room with a low sound. Peter wondered how Major Singh would go about getting the couple to exchange a kind word before parting, even sharing a kiss. But Major Singh was history and, after a final glance at his wife, Peter's father turned and marched from the kitchen. Peter heard the slam of the front door and the kitchen fell into silence. After a while, and when he had finished his breakfast, Peter, too, left, going through to the living room and turning on the TV to watch the cartoons he often did on Saturday mornings.

Peter thought of his father's initial question. He wasn't sure if he wanted to go out. Outside was a place of despair and danger. Even the weather was depressed, heavy grey covers instead of the electric blue and blanching sunshine of previous weeks, and Peter imagined the conferences of Covids behind the blanket of cloud, identifying their next victim and now unencumbered by the meddlesome boy from Number 15 New Cuttings Lane. Looking from the front window of the living room, Peter noticed that the Overlords hadn't even bothered to station any guards on the line this morning. He was no longer of importance.

He must have carried his depression with him like a pestilent air as his mother, with Julia in her arms, looked at him pointedly when he emerged into the kitchen once again.

'Are you not going to play in your den today then, Peter?' she asked kindly.

'I don't think so, Mum.'

'A bit of fresh air will do you good.'

'It looks like it's going to rain.'

'You can wear a jacket.'

'Maybe.'

'Look, Peter, I don't mind you playing outside. I just don't want you gallivanting around the place, and I certainly don't want you seeing Mr Singh again. He might be a harmless old man to you, but he might have Covid, I mean he could be…'

But she never finished. At that moment, a shaft of sunlight caught both mother and baby full on, pulling apart a gap in the dark clouds and revealing a skein of blue skies beyond. Mother and daughter were bathed in the strong light and his mother turned around instinctively to meet it, her face radiant in the projection.

'Look Peter,' she cried, turning the baby also in the direction of the sun, 'there's a rainbow over there, too.'

Peter moved closer to the pair and looked towards where his mother was pointing. The coloured lines almost split the sky, with the area to the outside of the rainbow still dark grey, while inside, closer to the horizon, the sky was clear with light. Peter followed the course of the rainbow's arc to where it met the earth and tried to imagine what it must be like underneath the colourful display, how lucky the people who lived there must be. It was as though his mother had been reading his thoughts.

'They say that there's treasure at the end of a rainbow,' she said.

'What type of treasure?'

'Gold, maybe.'

'Really?'

'Well, that's what people say, but I think it's just a means of saying your dreams will come true when you reach the end of the rainbow.'

'Oh.'

'That you should always keep hope in your heart, even when you can't see a way out.'

'That's good,' replied Peter calmly.

'Yes, it's the thing that keeps us all going. Having said that, it's not always easy. You still have to get to the end of the rainbow.'

'But that's not difficult? I can see it. Can't we just walk there?'

'Well, you could try, but...'

Again she was interrupted, this time by Julia erupting into a lung bursting cry, and Peter watched as his mother bolted into action, jigging around the kitchen and quietly reassuring the baby who, by degrees, stilled her sobs. When she was quiet once more, the pair re-joined Peter at the window, but the glorious parting in the clouds had disappeared, dragging with it the rainbow and the pulse of the unseen sun.

'Has it gone, Peter?' she asked.

'Yes, Mum.'

'Oh, that's a pity.'

'Yes.'

And both of them looked through the window, to where the band of beautiful colours had been just moments before.

*

Peter's father returned earlier than any of them had expected that afternoon, but if he had hoped to surprise his family with his premature arrival and a show of bonhomie, any goodwill had gone by the time he actually barged in through the kitchen door. Peter and his mother were both sitting at the table, starting on an apple each after their lunch.

'Is this yours?' he said forcefully, holding up a limp looking object in his hand.

'What is it?' his mother said. Her voice was neutral and non-committal.

'An old glove, I found it out the front.'

'Why would I leave a gardening glove lying at the front?'

'I don't know,' he said. 'I just asked the question.'

'Then I don't know,' she replied tersely, turning back to the table.

'Somebody's just gone past and left it out there. It's disgusting.' And with that, Peter's father put his toe on the pedal bin, ceremoniously dropping the object from a height into the container. The lid snapped shut.

But Peter knew who the green and white checked glove belonged to. He knew, too, why it had been left on their driveway. This was no careless disposal of an unwanted item. This was a signal. A message from Major Singh. The old man hadn't given up. The war was not yet over for the old warrior. But, as Peter finished swallowing the last section of apple, the question which really worried him was whether he, too, still had the stomach for the fight.

Chapter 16

It was a question he spent the rest of the day struggling with, lurking about his den. But even if he had wanted to, he could do nothing about it as his father was also in the garden, cutting the grass for what seemed like most of the afternoon. And although he didn't pay much attention to Peter, there was little chance of slipping away into the field, even if he had wanted to. And when his father had finished the grass, closing the wooden shed door with a resounding bang, he ventured down the garden and suggested a game of football. He sounded so reasonable, Peter felt he couldn't refuse, and in their one on ones of goalmouth action, Peter even found himself enjoying the game. His father seemed to have curbed his more competitive instincts, thinking more about his son. And in those moments, Peter loved his father. By the time they had finished, the shadows from the hedges had spread long across the garden. There was no chance he could disappear now, not when both parents would expect him inside.

*

Peter felt the melancholy of Easter Sunday even before he got up, lying in bed, considering everything that had happened recently, and listening to the muffled sounds of movement downstairs. It would be his mother, his father seldom rose early on a Sunday.

When he entered the kitchen, his mother turned and smiled, relieved maybe that it was him. Julia was in her pram next to the pine table and Peter went to greet her, poking his finger into the bundle of flesh and covers, thrilling when the baby grasped at his index finger. The radio was playing and it didn't take long for Peter to recognise it as a church service of some kind. It was unusual for either parent to listen to such a lengthy broadcast - the family couldn't be considered religious - and he looked at the radio with interest. His mother must have noticed, and when he turned away he saw that she was looking at him.

'It's the Easter service, from Canterbury,' she said simply.

Peter didn't reply, happy just to absorb the purposeful calmness of the voices and the morning light filling the kitchen. He already felt less agitated. After a while, his mother joined him at the table, taking his sister from the pram and cradling her in the small of her elbow, both apparently mesmerised by the liturgical voices from the radio. Peter glanced at his mother. She seemed in a trance, eyes focussed but not seeing on the pine cabinet set against the wall. Peter couldn't be sure if she was listening or not.

After he had served himself with cereal, the pieces clattering noisily into the bowl, Peter joined his mother in quiet contemplation of the radio. A man was speaking, his voice clear and sure.

'People right across the Globe feel the same uncertainty, fear, despair and isolation. But you are not alone.'

He could have been speaking directly to Peter. Ever since returning from Mr Singh's for the last time, he had felt a biting loneliness, born of impotence in the face of this crisis he had been unable to solve. Hearing the man tell him that he was not alone, that others felt the same way, made Peter feel better.

'Imagination, ambition, hope, are some of the foods that nourish our minds in dark times. Imaginative hope gives us a level-headed courage and a grand ambition when it is based on what we know to be true.'

Peter knew what was true. He had read about it, heard it from the blackbird and seen it with his own eyes. He knew, too, that this had given him courage to take on the Covids. And he had felt hope, just as his mother had done with the rainbow. But as the man continued, Peter reflected on what had become of that hope. Three times he had tried with Mr Singh to defeat the Covids. Three times they had failed, or rather, he had failed. Now he wasn't even allowed to see Mr Singh. Peter listened again and was surprised to hear his name mentioned.

'Not long after, Peter is telling Cornelius that Jesus had risen and that this was the foundation of hope for all people.'

Maybe that was the answer. Peter had heard the story about Jesus Christ before. They had been told it at school, in preparation for the visit to the Church, before the Covid mayhem began. It was incredible that a man could come back to life, but Mr Chambers had said it was true, so it must be. He had told them that Jesus had returned to save people, and for this reason, Jesus was the source of people's hope.

Peter drifted away from the voice, considering all he had just heard, sifting the messages through his own thoughts. But no answers came, only a nagging insistence that he needed help. And without Mr Singh, there was only one to turn to, the one who had started all this in the first place. The blackbird.

'Mum, can I go outside please?' His mother looked towards him, as if emerging from a dream.

'Yes, of course, love,' she said softly. 'Just make sure you stay in the garden.'

'Yes, Mum.'

'Good boy,' she smiled again and turned away, back to the radio, where all her answers seemed to be coming from.

The sun beamed strongly, as if making amends for being absent the previous day, and all the colours appeared washed and faded. In the harsh light, Peter felt more of a target than ever. There was no certainty that the Covids no longer took him seriously, and he was relieved to reach the covered protection of the den.

He glanced at the lower regions of the laurel hedge but there was no sign of the bird, and Peter began to wonder again if the creature had paid the price for informing on the Overlords. Knowing that he had been responsible for the death of the mother blackbird and her brood, would only add to his consternation.

'You have let us down little one.' The sound beat through the earth and air, and Peter jumped in surprise. There she was, almost close enough to touch, and just beyond his outstretched legs. Peter wondered how he had missed her appearance. One eye was turned towards him in enquiry, and inside the perfectly round rim of egg yolk yellow, it was difficult to tell where black pupil finished and brown iris began. It reminded Peter of Major Singh.

'I know,' Peter replied sombrely.

'We expected more of you.'

'I know, I tried.'

'You did, it is true, but now you have given up hope.'

'What else can I do? I have tried everything to get rid of the Covids. Nothing works.'

'So you have given up then?'

'Yes.'

'Did the disciples give up on Jesus?'

'No.'

'Would Major Singh give up?'

'I'm not allowed to see Major Singh.'

'Would Major Singh give up?'

'Didn't you hear me? I'll get in trouble if I try to see him again.'

'But what about the glove? The glove shows that Major Singh hasn't given up hope. Neither should you.'

'Mum says he's dangerous.'

'And what do you think? Do you think he is a danger?'

'I don't know.'

'Has he ever harmed you?'

'No, but school says we must be wary of strangers.'

'Major Singh is hardly a stranger now, though, is he?'

'No.'

'Then you know what you must do.'

'Yes, but…'

'Now!'

Peter looked away, despairing of the situation, of his choices, but when he looked back to where the blackbird had been, close to his feet, the creature was gone. Peter glanced towards the hedge, but she had disappeared completely. For a moment, Peter wondered if it had even been there at all.

Not that it mattered much now. The blackbird had been very clear, and Peter understood that he had no other choice. Hope had returned and one final effort was required. He would have to see Mr Singh.

But he would need to be swift. There was every chance his mother would lift from her reverie shortly. If he delayed, he might not have another opportunity. A glance towards the kitchen window was enough to confirm the coast was clear, and the dash along the field between the houses was swift. Peter could feel the sun-baked clay of the earth hard beneath his trainers.

When he arrived, Peter took in the whole garden with one glance. Major Singh wasn't there. He ran swiftly across the lawn, almost falling into the back door as he rapped on the PVC panel. The door opened slowly. If there was a moment of surprise in the old Sikh's face, it passed in an instant, replaced by a rueful smile. He was drying his hands with a grey dish towel and went to speak.

'You left the glove,' Peter blurted out, cutting off the old man.

'I did,' replied Major Singh, still smiling. 'I was worried about you. When you didn't come yesterday or the day before.'

'I wasn't allowed. Mum says I shouldn't see you again.'

'Ah, I see.'

'They say you're ill and dangerous.'

'Ah,' Mr Singh stopped, dropping one hand with the cloth to his side, and looking above Peter's head, considering. 'Maybe they're right. Maybe I'm not quite right in the head.'

'But I spoke to the blackbird,' Peter said, keen to carry on with his story. The old man had regathered himself.

'You did? And what did she say?'

'She said I should come and speak to you.'

'Anything else?'

'She said I shouldn't give up hope.'

'And she is right. You should never give up hope, young man, never, ever.'

'But Major Singh, nothing we've done has worked. The Covids are still here. They're all around, I've even seen them on your line. I'm just too young to do anything.'

'What rubbish! You're not too young. Look at Ranjit Singh, the mighty lion of the Punjab! He became head of the Sikhs when he was just nine years old. He was a great leader, a fearless horseman, just like you are on your bike. And he had to do it all with just one eye.'

'One eye?'

'Yes, little one, just the one eye, the Covids might have got the other one, I don't know. And then there was Gobind Singh, he became a guru when the same age as you as well. These men did great things for my ancestors. You, too, can be like them.'

'You think so?'

'I know so,' Major Singh said forcefully. 'You've just got to keep believing, keeping faith and hope that you'll find what you're looking for.'

'Like the disciples did with Jesus?'

'That's right. Exactly like Jesus. They kept believing and eventually Jesus came back to them.'

'Where did he come back to them, Major Singh?'

'Well, little one,' Major Singh paused, as if uncertain of how to continue. 'I'm afraid I'm not a Christian, so I couldn't say for sure. But I think it was probably in the cemetery where he had been buried.'

Peter seemed not to hear. 'Do you think they found him at the end of a rainbow?'

'At the end of a rainbow? Why?'

'Well, that's where you find things that you have been looking for.'

'Is that so? I thought all there was at the end of a rainbow was a pot of gold.'

'Well, that, too.'

'So you think that we also need to look at the end of the rainbow to find what we're looking for?'

'Yes.'

'To find a saviour, maybe made of gold?' The large Sikh ran one hand through his beard, smoothing the hairs.

'Yes, yes, that's right,' Peter responded eagerly. This was exactly the kind of idea he had been thinking about. 'A golden saviour. Someone to help us get rid of these Covids forever.'

'Hmm, a golden saviour, you say?'

'Yes!'

'To frighten away these Covids for good?'

'Yes!'

'I think I know what it might mean.'

'You do?'

'I might be wrong, though.'

'Come on, Major Singh, tell me,' Peter urged.

'Well,' began the Major slowly, fixing Peter with his stern eyes, 'I'd say that the thing we're looking for is...'

'Yes?'

'...probably a golden eagle.'

'A golden eagle?'

'Yes, they're enormous, and strike fear into the breasts of all other birds, even Electric Overlords. If anything can get rid of the Covids, it's one of those.'

'Really?'

'Yes,' the major paused, 'the trouble is, they're very rare.'

'Have you ever seen one?'

'Only once, in India, when I was your age. That was at the end of a long journey, and our family, too, had also almost given up hope of finding somewhere to settle. And then, this mighty creature appeared in the afternoon sky, swooping low over all of us refugees, and then a few hours later, we came to the city we had been looking for, and there we managed to make our lives.'

'And where can we find one, Major Singh?' Peter asked excitedly.

'I fear that will be very difficult, Peter-Sir.' For the first time, Major Singh sounded unsure.

'Why?'

'I don't think any are known to live around here.'

'But we must find one, we must!' insisted Peter, catching Mr Singh by his jacket and pulling at it, like a petulant child. The old man looked down at the boy, unsure what to say. Finally he spoke.

'I will do my best, Peter-Sir.'

'Oh, thank you, Major Singh, thank you,' cried Peter, oblivious to the hesitancy of the old man. 'You're the best!'

And without another word, Peter turned smartly, and ran to the bottom of the garden, leaping into the field and running home without stopping.

Chapter 17

The idea of the eagle didn't let him go for the rest of the morning, and as he sat close to his den, he looked up at the deep blue sky and imagined the creature gliding high and slow before swooping down at speed, scattering the terrified Covids or ripping them with its rasping talons. And when his imagination slowed, he drifted back inside the house and took his hopes to the Eye Pad, taking several attempts before he had approximated the spelling, but then marvelling at the photos of the birds, with their hooked beak and flared wings. And eyes which spoke of a reckoning. Peter liked how they were always solitary, a lone saviour to rescue the world. His calling on the creature's help would succeed where all else had failed.

As he grew more aware of how revenge and justice would look, so, too, did his anxiety to receive word of how Major Singh had got on. Peter didn't consider the details of how Mr Singh would obtain the creature, only that he would. He had promised, and Mr Singh wouldn't let him down. A hundred times he had to check the urge to slip over the edge of the garden and thrust along the field to Mr Singh's house. He wouldn't even need to speak to the old man. A signal would be enough. Enough to know whether the major had been successful or not.

But something always checked him. Major Singh had said the creatures were rare, uncommon in these parts. How easy would it really be to find one? And they were in the middle of lockdown, so nothing was normal, nothing straightforward. He should curb his impatience, give Mr Singh the time and space to achieve what was a difficult task. He knew, too, that if Mr Singh had some new information to impart, Peter would be the first to know. The glove would be left, a walk bye attempted. Peter even speculated whether Major Singh would dare follow his own footsteps along the field.

But as lunch came and went, and the shadows began to lengthen and fill the garden, and still there was nothing from the major, Peter realised his own opportunity for any kind of action was receding.

And when Peter could stand it no longer, and finally made the decision to go and see Mr Singh, it was too late. The sun was already below the horizon and he heard his father's voice, calling him inside, letting him know that he was expected for a bath, not in five minutes, not in half an hour, but this instant. After the bath would come dinner, and after that, there would be no chance of escape. It would have to be tomorrow.

Peter slept soundly but woke the following day taut with impatience. With the decision of whether to go or not already made, the persistent brakes of the family's morning routines frustrated him. He watched as his father had an easy breakfast, patiently answered his mother's enquiries about what he wanted on his toast, and tried hard not to ignore his baby sister in the cot. But all he wanted to do was bolt up to Mr Singh's house and see if he had acquired the eagle. He just hoped he was not too late. That he would arrive there breathless, only for the old man to casually state that the eagle had come and gone. 'Look Peter-Sir,' he would breezily declare, 'no Covids in sight. We have won!' And that would be the end of it.

The wait wasn't all bad. It gave Peter extra time, a space to be sure that he knew exactly what he was going to do when he got outside. That he would repeat the process that had served him so well. Lurking around the den until a gap in his mother's attention at the kitchen window allowed him to disappear over the edge, fly straight and fast as an arrow to Mr Singh's, and there receive the briefest of updates before retracing his steps with equal speed.

Only it didn't quite work out like that. Once outside, and just as he was at the edge of the field, his foot slipping down the slight incline, he heard his mother's voice from the house.

'Peter, have you got sun cream on?'

The day was ferociously hot, the sun starting the week with a burst of energy and determination. Peter glanced quickly up to the sun, down to his foot on the threshold, then turned reluctantly towards his mother. He walked slowly up the garden, his mind gradually filling with the powerful logic that there was nothing to stop his mother hailing him again for any random excuse. His previous transgression with Mr Singh hadn't been totally forgotten, and he realised he had been lucky, dead lucky, with his previous forays up the field. He couldn't be sure such fortune would hold again. He needed a change of plan. By the time his mother had finished liberally smearing him with the white cream he had something.

'Mum, can I go on my bike please?' Peter said, perched at the doorway, unwilling to go any further into the kitchen. He wanted to be off more than ever.

His mother hesitated, carefully observing her son, weighing her responses. Peter knew more was required.

'I promise not to talk to anyone, Mum. Please, please,' he whined.

'OK, love, but make sure you stay this end of the road, and no talking to anyone. Understood?'

'Yes, Mum.'

He swiftly removed the bike from the shed, and was on the road in an instant, his legs fuelled by the thought that he might already be too late, that the eagle had done its business and the Covids were long gone. A feeling which only grew as he cycled along the asphalt surface, parallel to the thick coil of wire, which was bare its entire length. Indeed, the hot air seemed to have burnt all life from the familiar route. He passed no cars, saw no humans and even the growing tendrils on the canes at the front of Mr Singh's garden were stilled in the breezeless day. It was like an eerie no-man's land, and Peter couldn't decide if he felt disappointed or frightened when Mr Singh didn't immediately appear as he slowed his bicycle in front of the old man's house. But the house remained silent and Peter turned slowly at the start of the dirt track with a strange feeling he struggled to explain. For the sake of appearances, he cycled back the length of the road, stopping briefly at his own home, hoping to attract the attention of his mother, a show of trustworthiness. But he didn't stay long, keen to be back in front of

Mr Singh's house, to maximise the chances of attracting the old man's attention.

As he went past Mrs Proudfoot's, Peter thought he saw a shadow pass behind the gauze of the front window, but it was gone in a moment, and might have been a trick of the light. As Peter reached the old man's house, he stopped pedalling, letting the bike's inertia pull it towards the junction of the dirt track. Again, there was no movement from within the building, and again Peter was forced to wearily retrace his route back up the lane.

Three times he repeated the process, his legs a little slower, his heart a little heavier on each pass. He knew what an easy solution would be. Descend from his bike, sprint quickly to the front door and knock vigorously. The old Sikh would notice that, for sure. But any encounter made would still be in sightline of Mrs Proudfoot's property. And Peter had given his mother his word. No talking to strangers. On his bike, he could still make his excuses. Once off it, he would have nothing.

On the fourth trip, it happened. Peter saw the front door swing reluctantly open, the old man barely looking up as he stepped gingerly onto the driveway. His lightweight gardening clothes had returned, and Peter watched carefully as the old man made slow progress over the stones of the driveway in front of the garage, and for a moment the image of the major holding the scarecrow and storming across the lawn came to Peter. The contrast couldn't have been greater.

But Mr Singh, and the answer, were still coming and Peter's tension rose as the old Sikh drew closer, lifting his head and offering a weak smile by way of greeting.

'Have you found him yet, Mr Singh?' Peter almost shouted. The old man paused, went to say something, stopped, and then began again, his voice low and serious.

'No, Peter-Sir, I'm afraid not. I've been looking hard, but nothing.'

'Oh.'

'Maybe we should try something else? The scarecrow maybe?'

Peter noticed the strain in the old man's voice, but he was already struggling with the news that the golden saviour hadn't been found. Peter was numb and the old man was speaking once more.

'Or maybe we could try some loud music? Set up the stereo here on the lawn, wait till the Covids are all on the line, then blast them full volume. That will work, won't it, Peter-Sir? Peter-Sir?'

But Peter wasn't listening. He could only stare at the old man. At no point had he thought Mr Singh wouldn't find the eagle.

'I know, I know,' cried the old man enthusiastically. 'This is bound to work. We used them all the time in India to scare birds away from the crops. Firecrackers. Yes, yes, a loud bang and we'll put the fear of God into these Overlords. They won't even dream of perching on this wire again, that's for sure.'

Peter was silent, looking down at his hands splayed on the handlebars, thinking. When he lifted his head once more, he looked directly into the old man's eyes.

'No, Mr Singh,' Peter started, low and measured. 'It must be the golden one. Nothing else will work.'

The old man held Peter's gaze and the only sound was the faint moan of a car accelerating in the distance.

'Then I will try to find it,' Mr Singh said softly.

'When?'

'Soon.'

*

But 'soon' couldn't come soon enough. Peter only realised it when he had returned home, dropped the bike on the grass in front of the back window, smiled at his mother, then drifted down the garden. Was 'soon' five minutes or fifty? Or maybe five hours, or would it take Major Singh five days to track down this elusive emperor of the skies? How many more times would he have to listen to the evening news talk about hundreds of people dying? 'Soon' was only a word, and words, like promises, were getting cheap. It was a conviction that only grew stronger as Peter watched the sun trace its way across the sky and begin its slow westward descent, spreading warm light over bushes and trees, but signalling to Peter that nothing was happening. That no golden eagle was appearing, and 'soon' just wasn't going to do it.

But if Major Singh had failed, one option remained. The one person he knew he could rely on. If he had enough courage. He knew what he was looking for. He knew, too, where to go. After all, his mother had showed him the right direction, and he had seen the point on the horizon where he must head towards.

And so, as the sun began its final play with the horizon and the upper layer of hedges in the garden turned the colour of burnished copper, Peter stood up, making himself tall and determined. With a final look towards the kitchen window, now flashing the reflection of the dying sun, Peter slipped over the edge of the garden, into the field and began running hard through the thigh length corn, the ears of which were just beginning to reveal themselves.

*

'Hello, love' he said, pushing the door to the kitchen with his shoulder before placing the two plastic bags of shopping onto the floor beside the table. 'I got the shopping you wanted.'

But the woman paid no attention to the shopping, instead looking at her husband, hard and direct.

'Have you seen Peter?' she said.

The man narrowed his eyes. His wife looked worn and tense, and he sensed a confrontation. He didn't want to argue, now. The truth was he never wanted to argue, but he had to defend himself, and she had grown so unpredictable. Nothing like the accommodating beauty he had met outside that nightclub nearly a decade ago now. But he didn't want to jump to conclusions. He would be cautious in his reply.

'No, why?'

'He's not in the garden, or in his room. I thought he might be out on the street somewhere.'

'Is his bicycle here?'

'Yes, it's out the back.'

'Oh.'

There was a moment of silence. The situation was unprecedented. Something which threatened both of them. It was a time for unity.

'I thought you might have passed him coming up the street. I couldn't see him the other way. I didn't want to leave Julia by herself to look.'

'I didn't see anyone on the street,' he said, drawing closer to his wife whose eyes looked bleary and bloodshot. He placed a hand gently on her elbow, but she might not have noticed. Then he moved quickly, first to the back door, and from there into the garden.

'Peter, peter!' he yelled, pausing between each word. When there was no response he came back inside, passing his wife and disappearing upstairs. She could hear the sound of doors opening and closing before he came down once more. Now it was his turn to look grim.

'He might have gone to see that old man again?' she ventured. She could see he, too, was shocked.

'What, the old Indian chap at the end?'

'Yes.'

'I see.'

'I'll call Mrs Proudfoot,' she said.

Her mobile phone was on the table and she sat down to dial. The man watched as she put the phone flat to her ear. There were no formalities.

'Mrs Proudfoot, have you seen Peter? He's gone missing.'

A pause. The woman's eyes stared ahead, unseeing.

'When was this? Before lunch?'

Another pause.

'Were there just the two of them?'

The man looked on as his wife responded in low murmurs to the unfolding narrative at the other end.

'And then Peter rode back? Did you see him later at all?'

After a further short spell of intense listening, the conversation was nearly over.

'Ah, I see. Thank you, Mrs Proudfoot. Yes, of course we'll call you if we need more help. Thank you.' The woman placed the phone slowly on the table and turned to her standing husband.

'She saw Peter talking to the man this morning, when he was out on his bike. But she's seen nothing since.'

The man snatched his car keys from the table. 'Right,' he said with an uneasy mix of determination and fear. 'Let's see what the old bugger has to say for himself.'

The unnecessary trip in the car took under a minute, the man parking his car at the final stretch of asphalt, blocking the way for other vehicles to pass. But he was beyond such considerations. He was on a mission, a man whose son's life was endangered. He ground his way across the stones of the gravel drive, and his knuckles struck the composite door firmly.

It wasn't long before a dark figure flashed before the window closest to the door, and a moment later a large Sikh was standing in front of him. The younger man noticed how his considerable size filled much of the space, and his turban almost touched the upper frame.

'What have you done with my boy?' the visitor demanded, his petulance ebbing in the face of the larger man.

But the old man didn't reply, just staring calmly at the visitor, as if assessing him. In the end he spoke, his voice deep and formal.

'Mr Lassiter, I presume?'

'Yes, didn't you hear me? I want to know what's happened to my boy, Peter.'

'Peter was here this morning,' the old man said simply.

'Yes, I know. But now he's disappeared. Have you touched him?'

'Touched him?' the man's eyebrows lifted in enquiry. 'Mr Lassiter. I can assure you, I know nothing about your son's disappearance.'

'What were you talking to him about then?' demanded the man.

'What your son and I discuss is, I'm afraid, between ourselves only.'

'You what?' The conversation wasn't turning out as he had imagined.

'I think you heard me very clearly.'

'You'd better not have touched him or...'

'Or what, Mr Lassiter?' The old man's coal black eyes never wavered from the other's.

'I'm going to call the police,' the man said, but without conviction.

The Sikh's eyes narrowed in appreciation of this new information, and a troubling silence fell between the two men.

'Do what you must, Mr Lassiter, but now, you will leave my property. I have nothing further to offer.'

The other man hesitated. The interview had been inconclusive. No answers had been furnished and he was unsure what to say.

'Go, Man, I say!' the Sikh shouted, edging forwards and forcing the younger man to turn abruptly, walking quickly away, not quite in a straight line.

But the older man didn't close the door, or go inside. Instead, he watched the retreating figure, back to his car, following him with slow swivel of his head as the hapless man placed his car into reverse and drove beyond the privet hedge. There he stood for some time, watching the corner where man and vehicle had gone, considering. Then he stepped beyond the threshold, closing and locking the door behind him before walking over to the garage, bending low to flip the large door panel. When it was fully open, he disappeared into the darkness inside. The panel remained open and, for a few moments, a stillness returned to the early evening warmth.

Chapter 18

He had stopped running hard by the middle of the field, and by the time he came to the track at the far end, he had slowed to a walk, grateful for the rest. He had only been dimly aware of the track's existence previously, seen from the distance of their house it had always held a half-life, the place where his enemies would muster before their final skirmish across the field towards his den. Maybe he had also walked along this way with his parents. With the sun almost down, it was difficult to grasp anything specific.

The path cut across his line of travel and he was tempted to follow it for a while, the safe option maybe. But his objective lay straight ahead, not to either side. He had already told himself that courage and boldness would be needed – deviation was a sign of weakness, and he was angry with himself for even considering it. So, he scuffed his feet across the dry mud of the path and plunged into the adjacent field, confident in the fading light that he was still heading in the correct direction.

He walked for another ten minutes in the stillness of dusk, brushing his fingers across the tops of the emerging ears of wheat and scanning across the field from one hedgerow to another. He wondered at what point and from where the eagle would emerge, and was surprised he hadn't considered such details before.

He was still looking when the field gave way quite suddenly to a small road. In the half light, it looked as though someone had dribbled an inky trail through the countryside, and the smooth asphalt under his feet felt novel after the uneven layers of the field. It felt good to reconnect with the human world again. He could see no more fields immediately beyond the road, instead, a ditch gave way to some sort of compound, with shanty walls of wooden slats and chicken wire, inside of which Peter could just make out the haphazard movements of wild fowl of some kind, geese maybe. It didn't matter, Peter would no longer be able to continue his dogged pursuit in the same line. He would have to traverse the road for a bit, until he could renew his original course.

But the decision of which way to go was difficult. Peter knew that the wrong way now could mean missing the thread of his original thrust. After a little reflection, he plumped for left. As he took his first steps, he thought of home, instinctively looking to his side, from where he had come. But he could see nothing beyond the rise of the field, and in the rapidly enveloping gloom he felt something dry up inside him.

He wandered rather than walked along the road, still not convinced that he had made the right decision, half looking out for the appearance of the golden saviour, half listening to the night scratchings that were making themselves heard along the quiet lane. After a few hundred yards, he came to a sinuous bend in the road. An overgrown track lay to the left, in the direction of where he had come from, while a little beyond, shearing off to the right, a track climbed in a gentle rise between fields. Peter could see the silhouette or a large oak tree where the path met the crest of the field. It wasn't in exactly the same direction he had been following previously, but it wasn't far off. Walking a way up the path, he would soon be able to cut across a field again, picking up the old route.

But Peter wasn't sure he wanted to walk amongst crops any more. Each field was now a sea of black, and he imagined each stalk coming to life in the dark, whispering to themselves about him as he walked through. He doubted they would be kind to the trespasser.

As he made his way off the road, into the hard rut made by generations of tractors, Peter felt the chill of the air for the first time. He only had a T-shirt below his sweatshirt, the sleeves of which he now made sure were fully pulled down. He hoped the eagle would come to him soon.

From far away he heard a motorbike accelerating, but when he looked back towards the road, he could see no lights at all, neither from the motorbike, streetlight or any house. In the west, almost all light had slipped from the sky, a time which Peter always associated with dinner. But today he would not be at home, and he knew his mother would be worried. Wondering where he could possibly be, what had happened to him.

Only the eagle kept him going. It was the only thing he had left, and he knew he must pursue it beyond his anxiety. Only the golden one could strike fear into the Overlords and force them off the lines. In the darkness of the track, he pictured their demise. Firstly, the eagle would guide Peter back home, hovering above him like a kite on a string. Then, once within range of the coarse electric wire, the eagle would soar high before dropping swiftly onto the Covids, scattering them and setting off a chain reaction of startled crows across the country. It would be like a trail of dominoes falling. All he had to do was find the eagle.

But Peter could see little further than his own shadowy footsteps now, and the track was petering out as it passed one field entrance after another, and it wasn't long before the track terminated completely, merging into a field with a low growing crop. Peter didn't even bother to bend down to investigate what it was. It didn't matter now. He just wanted to be out of this field. He could go back, he knew. But it was over ten minutes to the road, and in the wrong direction. He had to go on, even though, for the first time in his adventure, Peter recognised the movement of his own fear.

It was a feeling which only grew as he began his crossing of the anonymous field, stumbling in the darkness, his hand making contact with the cold, undefined matter on the ground. And when he raised his hand to assess the damage, it was no longer visible. He walked quicker as a result, afraid now of the unseen vastness surrounding him and the transformation which comes about with the coming of night. Vague things from the underworld, seeping up through the cracks in the dry earth, feeling the pull of the darkness, which gave them cover from the heat and light of the day. An ecosystem of spirits. It was another world, like his own, or that of his parents, but different. There were, Peter suddenly realised, many worlds, and he had just been living in one of them.

Five minutes later, he had reached another road, and he realised that for the whole time he had been in the field, not once had he thought of the eagle. Something had broken in the crossing and, as his foot hit the hard tarmac, Peter realised what he wanted, more than anything, was to be home. But he no longer knew where home was and, looking around wildly, he could no longer be sure from which direction he had even come from.

The road was similar to the previous one, little more than an ancient track connecting distant granges that had been covered in asphalt in homage to the motor car. As he could see no lights in either direction, it hardly mattered which way he turned. But there was still agony in his final choice of left. What if heading right would, by some miracle, take him home within minutes?

The night air was thick and he felt sure it was already past his bed time. But he felt a long way from the thrill of an eight year old staying up late. He was very cold now, but instead of rousing himself to warmth by speeding up, he kept a slow, reluctant shuffle, unsure if he was just moving further away from where he needed to be. All he could hear was the rasp and clunk of his lazy feet on the artificial surface. It was like a march of doom.

He heard the sound of the engine first, but it wasn't until the branches of the hazel and blackthorn of the hedgerow beside him had flashed into life from the errant headlamps, did Peter realise that the car was actually heading towards him. On the gently winding road, he still had a few seconds to decide how to respond. He went with his first instinct, scurrying to the side of the road, pressing himself between the thin saplings which bordered the ditch, and ducking down low, turning his back to the lights which swept back and forth as the car approached. The appearance of the vehicle had returned him immediately to his own world, a world in which he had run away from home, disobeyed both parents, a world in which punishment for transgression was imminent. Hiding away might delay that reckoning.

When he felt caught in the whole force of the harsh beam, he squeezed himself tighter, hoping that he was sufficiently concealed to avoid detection, or be mistaken for thrown away rubbish. The car passed noisily and Peter held himself rigid, readying himself for the sound of deceleration. But there was no change from the car's engine, only the gradual fade of the departing vehicle. He kept low and still until he could hear no more and, only then, as he stretched his legs and emerged onto the hard surface did he begin to wonder if he had done the right thing. He had acted on a childish impulse, he knew, but maybe the time to be acting as a child had passed. He wondered how long it would be before he had a similar chance.

And so, as he resumed his slow walk into the darkness, worry joined hunger, fatigue and cold, taking him further away from the search for the eagle and the world of the Electric Overlords. He thought of his mother, and little Julia, of how much he would like to be on the carpeted floor in the living room, rolling around and letting his baby sister climb all over him, and then watching the delight in his mother's face as both exploded into smiles and giggles. But all that felt a long way off now.

Suddenly, he saw the flashing lights of another car, quicker this time, but still well beyond the tight bend which Peter had just come around. This time he would stand still to be seen. His quest was over. He would accept whatever punishment corresponded with his flight. Somehow the search for the eagle, the threat of the Overlords and conversations with the blackbird, none of them were quite as real as the present. The Covids had terrified him, but this, this walk into darkness, was something beyond.

He felt himself pinned by the headlights of the car as it swooped around the bend, hardly yielding in speed, and Peter twisted his head away from the dazzling beam, confident that the driver would still see the whole extent of his body. He was impossible to miss by the side of the road. But as the seconds passed, there was no let-up in the engine's whine, and it was only after the car had passed, almost sucking the air out of the night, did Peter wonder how close he had come to actually being struck by the vehicle. But it was a secondary consideration, coming long after the surprise and shock at not being detected. What kind of adult drives straight past a child alone at night?

With the car's sudden passing, the blackness of the night came more forcefully than ever, like the lid of a tomb falling on a person still living. In the darkness, Peter found it impossible to fight off the questions. How many more cars would follow this obscure route this late? And which of those would even stop? Had the passage across the field affected him in some way, merged him with the spirits of the night, making him invisible to the human world? If he had crossed to the other side, how was he to even return?

He was hardly aware of his steps now, his body numb, and all his senses coagulating into an unthinking desperation. It was shocking. They might not even find his body, so remote was this location.

When the next car came, Peter barely knew how much longer he had been walking for, and at first Peter looked at the brightening scene of black tarmac and tangled hedgerows without understanding. Instinctively, he drifted to one side, like a tramp making way, not even bothering to turn around to look. It was only as the car drew to his side, slowing to his pace, did Peter begin to realise what was happening.

'Have you found what you are looking for, little one?' The voice was unmistakeable, syrupy and strange.

'Major Singh!' cried Peter, unable to move, or stop the tears which had risen, fast and hard. The next thing he knew, the car had stopped completely, a door opened, and his arms were around the old man, pressing himself tightly to the old man's chest and feeling the gentle touch of the large Sikh's hands on the back of his head.

'He's not here,' Peter sniffled, easing himself away from the major. 'I thought he'd be here, at the end of the rainbow. But he's not, he's not here…' And with that Peter buried his head once more into the major who stood silent, cradling the boy in the darkness. After a while, the old man spoke.

'Come, Peter-Sir, get in. It's time to get you home.'

Neither man nor boy spoke at first, both drawing comfort from the silence and the presence of the other. It was Peter who broke the spell.

'I couldn't find the golden eagle, Major Singh,' he said. 'I thought he would be at the end of the rainbow, where the gold is, where the things are that you really wish for. But he wasn't there.'

In the darkness of the car, the old man waited before turning to Peter with a smile.

'Don't give up, little one. He will appear.'

'When?'

'How do you know he wasn't above you all the time? In fact, how do you think I found you?'

Peter was surprised. This was something which he hadn't thought about. But before he could ask Mr Singh any more, the car had made the familiar turn into the street where both lived. The journey back had taken much less time than Peter had expected. He thought he had walked many miles from home, but the trip back in the warmth of the car had taken minutes.

The old Sikh knocked firmly on the door, then stood back, a few paces behind Peter, now draped in a blanket the old man had produced as they had parked in Peter's driveway.

When she opened the door, Peter's mother took several seconds to absorb the scene before her, each of them static in the sodium light above the entrance. Then she moved forwards, wrapping her child in her arms and pulling him close. Peter gave way once more to a turbulent mix of emotions. As her relief receded she looked up to the Sikh, who hadn't moved.

'What have you done with him?' she said angrily.

'I found the boy on the back road to Fassingham,' said Mr Singh flatly.

'Did you take Peter? Mrs Proudfoot said she had seen you leaving by car, shortly after my husband saw you. What did you do with him?'

'Mrs Proudfoot, ah, well, that is no surprise,' said the old man, more to himself, before continuing, 'but I just went out to find

Peter. I had an idea where he might be. It is the Overlords, Mrs Lassiter.'

'The what?'

'The Overlords, on the line, the Covids, who are doing all this.'

'I have no idea what you are talking about.'

'Peter hasn't told you about the Electric Overlords, then?' Mr Singh stepped forward, putting a hand gently on Peter's shoulder. 'Peter, go inside now.'

'Yes, Mr Singh,' replied Peter, looking up for the first time. Peter's mother stared at the pair before shifting aside.

'Go to your room, Peter, and get changed into your pyjamas. Are you hungry?'

'Very hungry, Mum.'

'Go on now, I'll be with you shortly.'

Without looking back, Peter slipped past his mother, still wrapped inside the warmth of the blanket from the old man's car. Peter's mother closed the door behind him, then turned to the large Sikh waiting patiently on the gravel driveway.

'The Electric Overlords, Mrs Lassiter…'

'Yes…?'

Chapter 19

Peter woke the following day with sore throat, headache and a deep emptiness, which he didn't even try to explain to himself as he spent much of the next two days in bed. It was only as the physical pains eased, that he began to allow the sensations and perspective to return. He was just an eight year old boy with an idea which had failed miserably. He had found only humiliation in his flight across the fields.

He was troubled, too, at his parents' reaction. Neither mentioned his escapade when they visited him in his room, his mother only encouraging him to sit up and hold firmly the tray upon which the bowl of soup was balanced, asking him how he felt, and if he wanted to go downstairs to watch television. But not a word about his night-time adventure. It was as though they were deliberately overlooking it, that talking about it would resurrect whatever demons had possessed him in the first place.

But they weren't demons, only childish things, and by the time he felt well enough to come downstairs to watch television on the third day, Peter, too, wondered what he had been so sure about. After breakfast, sitting in the comfortable sofa watching cartoons, Peter started to make his plans of old, he would drift down to his den after lunch, sweep the floor and make sure the pegs he used to hold down the edges hadn't been pulled up. Then he would scan the horizon, alert to any sign of his old enemies advancing across the fields towards him. He only half thought of the blackbird, and what she might say if she appeared.

It was around mid-morning when he heard the knock on the front door. But he made no move. His mother was in the kitchen with Julia and the glass door which led to the hallway was open, and he soon heard the sound of her slippers slapping across the parquet floor. A moment later, the front door opened but Peter paid no attention to the low voices he could just hear above the whoops and groans of the cartoon he was watching. It would be an adult thing.

He was surprised therefore when his mother put her head around the living room door, looking brightly at him.

'Peter, it's Mr Singh. He wants to speak with you.'

'Major Singh?'

Peter wasn't sure he wanted to see Mr Singh. Not because he didn't wish to, but because he had failed him so spectacularly. They had been a team, but he had tried taking matters into his own hands, and come up short. He had let Mr Singh down.

'Is he here now?'

'Yes, Peter.'

Peter hesitated. It was strange for the old man to come to his house. Odder still that his mother should be the willing messenger. But he didn't really have much choice, and a part of him knew he had unfinished business with the strange Indian.

He flicked the TV off with the remote control and plodded to the door. Peter felt the colour rising to his face when he saw the Sikh, waiting patiently at the doorway. As he approached, his mother backed away, leaving the two of them alone, Mr Singh a step down but still taller than Peter.

'Peter-Sir, how are you?'

'Better, thanks.'

'Peter-Sir, I have news. I have found the golden eagle.'

Peter could hardly believe what he was hearing and, like the waters behind a breaking dam, all his previous hopes came back to him. It seemed like an age before he was able to respond.

'Really?'

'Yes, I think so. He is to come this evening, at dusk, just before seven, can you be there?'

'I don't know. I don't think I'm allowed out.'

'Ask your mother. If she agrees, come to me, to the front door, I'll be waiting.'

'Yes, Major Singh.'

'Good boy. Tonight, Peter-Sir, we truly will defeat these Covids. I am sure of it!'

'Yes, Major Singh,' Peter cried, suddenly caught up in the old man's enthusiasm.

After he had closed the door, he waited in the hallway. He was hesitant to ask his mother, after all that had happened. But the major had suggested it, and if she said no, well, that would be the end of it.

Still, it wasn't easy, and as he stood in front of her in the kitchen, he found his mouth drying, his request emerging weak and scratchy. His mum stayed quiet for a long time, looking at him intently. He almost wished he hadn't asked.

'Yes, Peter. You can go,' she said finally. 'But make sure you come straight back here when you have finished with Mr Singh.'

'Yes, Mum. I will,' replied Peter. And he meant it. He was astonished at this license, and he was determined this time not to let anyone down, least of all his mother. He was tempted to tell her about Major Singh's find, but he held back. It was enough that she would let him go.

The evening couldn't come quickly enough, and his play in the den after lunch was distracted, laced with considerations of the eagle; what it would look like, from where it would come, and how the Covids would respond. Peter was grateful to his mother for the early dinner, but struggled not to gobble the meal.

'Chew your food, Peter,' his mother chided, 'or you'll end up choking yourself before you even get to Mr Singh's.'

Peter looked up and smiled, but couldn't completely wipe away his puzzlement. It was as though she were encouraging him.

At five to seven, Peter was on the driveway, hands tightly gripping the handlebar of his bike. It would take him seconds to be at Mr Singh's but he didn't want to be late. His mother was with him, Julia in her arms, and it was she who finally gave the signal.

'Ok, Peter, it's time to go. Ride carefully, and come straight back.'

'Yes, Mum.'

'Keep to the side if a car comes.'

'Yes, Mum.'

'I love you, Peter.'

'I love you too, Mum.'

There was still light in the sky and the day had kept its heat, like a long summer's evening. The breeze felt refreshing on his face as he built up speed, his spinning legs reflecting his mounting excitement. It was only when he stopped the furious whirl of his legs, letting the bike cruise to a stop in front of the privet hedge of Major Singh's house that Peter looked up towards the line for the first time. In his excitement about the arrival of the eagle, he had forgotten about the Covids.

Two of them greeted him, the profile of their jagged feathers appearing against the rich evening sky as they bobbed back and forth. Peter thought of them sucking up the electricity swirling along the line, feeding every part of their black bodies, and giving them the extra strength to launch fresh attacks on humankind. The sight of the black sentinels brought everything back to him; the warnings of the blackbird, their efforts to defeat the Overlords, his failures. All leading up to this moment. It was overwhelming and, returning his gaze to the road, he was glad to see Major Singh waiting for him at the entrance to the drive.

Peter was surprised to see how smart he looked, with broad slacks, brown leather shoes, and a pressed white shirt, the collars of which overlapped a smart jacket. The folds of his black turban were sharp and straight.

'Major Singh,' Peter said, by way of greeting.

'Good evening, Peter-Sir,' replied the old man, taking hold of one handle of Peter's bike. 'Are you ready?'

'Oh yes, Major Singh.'

'Good. This will be a historic moment. The day we finally defeat the Electric Overlords.'

'Yes, Major Singh.'

'Come, leave your bike here, we shall go to the front of the house and wait there until more Covids appear. Then I shall summon the golden saviour.'

But before Peter had time to answer, another voice rang out in the twilight.

'Mr Singh, step away from that boy, this instant!'

Man and boy turned to see Mrs Proudfoot, walking towards them in the middle of the road.

'You're an evil man, Singh. It's disgusting what you're doing with this boy. Let him go, now. I'm calling his mother.'

Mrs Proudfoot had continued towards them and was no more than a few yards from the astonished pair. Even the Covids looked down from the line. The old Sikh was the first to recover.

'Mrs Proudfoot, this is none of your business.'

'None of my business, none of my business?' she screeched. 'You abduct this boy a few days ago, and now you're back with him! I'm calling the police.'

The man continued staring at the woman, whose face contorted with the strain of her outrage. Then, very gently, he turned to Peter, bending to talk quietly to the boy.

'Peter, put your bike down and go stand by the front door. I will be with you shortly.'

Peter felt the pat on his back from the large man as he settled the bike on the fence by the side of the driveway, before starting the slow walk to the front of the man's house. As he walked he heard Mrs Proudfoot's hysterical shout once more.

'Peter, Peter, don't go. Come back! If you don't…'

But she never finished, her voice dying like the last drops of water down a drain. Peter turned to see the large man with one hand clasped around the woman's throat, poised and calm, as he exerted pressure on Mrs Proudfoot's windpipe.

'Mrs Proudfoot, do you know what your neck reminds me of?'

But Mrs Proudfoot was in no position to speak, her eyes bulged in fear and disbelief, and Peter realised she must be being raised onto her toes by the old man.

'It reminds me of the chickens my father and I used to dispatch, before plucking and eating them. First we squeezed, and then twisted their necks. The quicker the better. Do you hear me, Mrs Proudfoot?'

Mrs Proudfoot might have responded with her eyes, but she made no sound. The old man was speaking once more.

'Now, you will leave us alone, completely alone. In a while the boy will return home. Safely. Call his mother if you are truly concerned, which I doubt. Do you understand that Mrs Proudfoot? Just nod.'

Peter saw the slightest movement of the woman's head, her grey hair falling about her face. She sagged as Mr Singh released his grip, and Peter thought she would fall to the ground. But she was still, remaining where she was, looking forward but without seeing as the old man turned and rejoined Peter.

'Peter-Sir,' the major began, 'I apologise for my behaviour. But I couldn't stomach the woman's suspicions and accusations, coming to my house and...' but the old man stopped, looking down at Peter, considering. 'But that isn't your battle, is it, Peter-Sir? We have more important things to think about, the future of all mankind. Isn't that so, Peter-Sir?' Even in the dying light, Peter could see the gleam in the old man's dark eyes.

'Oh, yes, Major Singh. Where is the golden eagle?'

'Come, Peter-Sir. Come, we will wait at the front of the house. I'm sure he will be here soon. If we are lucky, more Covids will come, too.'

The pair scrunched over the stones of the driveway until they reached the path around the house. There, both man and boy slipped down, resting their backs against the whitewashed wall, looking towards the electricity line, now black and featureless in the evening light. Mrs Proudfoot had fled and the two Covids had been joined by a third, and Peter watched as occasionally one would fall from the wire, almost like a stone, a strong flap of the wings before reaching the ground. Something between the row of sweet peas and the privet hedge seemed to be attracting them, but in the shadows it was impossible to make out what. Neither said very much as the minutes past, and Peter realised he was just happy to sit there, in silence next to his friend. As they waited, a few more Covids arrived, silhouettes only now against the dark sky.

'When is the golden eagle coming, Major Singh,' whispered Peter, looking hopefully up towards the old man.

'Soon, Peter. Any time soon. In fact,' Major Singh pulled up the cuff of his jacket and looked at his watch, 'it should be here any moment now.'

'Oh,' Peter replied. Major Singh had rekindled his hopes, and he wasn't sure he would be able to take disappointment again. He looked once more towards the line.

Suddenly, he felt a nudge to his side.

'Look, Peter-Sir,' said Major Singh, gesturing to his right, high above the garage. 'Can you see it?'

At first, Peter could see nothing, but as his eyes focussed on the gloom, a shape appeared, planing smoothly through the darkening skies, similar to how Peter had seen in the videos, an effortless procession through the air.

'It's the eagle, Major Singh!' Peter cried, struggling to control his excitement.

'Yes, Peter,' the old man said softly. 'It is. The golden one.'

And both watched as the creature arced through the sky in front of the Sikh's house, an occasional beat of its tear shaped wings taking it forwards, letting it float through the air. Slowly it went out, beyond them and across the field of grassland opposite, reaching the furthest extent of the fallow land, before banking in a lazy curve and returning. Peter watched the creature intently as it straightened towards them. In the gloom, the creature seemed smaller than Peter had remembered from the videos, but it may have been a trick of the light. There was nothing false about what the bird did next, losing height and making straight for the wire where the Covids still perched. In the shadows, Peter gripped Major Singh's hand. This was the moment. The creature came hurtling down, an occasional long, lush beat of its wings, but for the most part it held them outstretched, slicing through the twilight.

And then, as it was almost upon them, the black shapes lifted from the line, scattering with a raucous calling which scared and thrilled Peter in equal measure. Here was the climax of all their efforts, and Peter watched as the eagle passed serenely between the frightened Covids and, just as quickly, it was above them, Peter twisting his head to catch the creature, as it disappeared over the roof of the house, with barely space to spare.

For a few moments, neither said anything and all Peter could hear was the fading cries of the startled Covids, whose visible forms had already dissolved into the blackness of the night.

'We did it, Major Singh,' said Peter eventually, looking up at the old man who was smiling.

'Yes, Peter, we did. The Electric Overlords will come no more.'

'Really?'

'Truly, Peter. It is the end. Soon word will go out that no wire is safe for long. It is over.'

Peter leant across and clumsily wrapped his arms around the old man, and in the final embers of light, man and boy became one in the shadows.

'Now, go home quickly, Peter,' Major Singh said, lifting himself with difficulty from the concrete path. 'And remember to thank your mother for letting you come.'

But Peter's heart was so full of joy that the old man's words were forgotten by the time he arrived home. He wasn't even surprised to see his mother waiting on the driveway for him, her smile widening as he approached.

Chapter 20

Harpreet Singh Kapur watched as the young boy pedalled furiously away, the bike swaying from side to side with the excitement the child took with him. He chuckled to himself. He felt he had done something good.

Straining, he could just make out Peter's mother, waiting at the entrance of her driveway. He thought he saw her raise her arm in salute as the boy reached her, but his eyes might have failed him. Never mind. He was glad he had spoken with her, explained what had happened, and that she had understood. He couldn't have done it without her help, and he doubted he would have reached a similar agreement with the father.

He turned and walked slowly across the drive, to the passage between the house and the shed. The natty little man was waiting where he had been instructed to, well out of sight, beyond the back door. The creature had already been put away, and Harpreet Singh could see the hooked beak and flat face of the owl behind the plastic bars of the case the man held. The man appeared keen to leave.

'I hope that was what you wanted,' the man said.

'It was fine,' Mr Singh replied curtly. He drew closer to the man, who shrank a little in the presence of the large Sikh, and handed him a plain white envelope. 'Here is the remainder of what I owe.'

He knew he had paid well over the odds for the unusual request. But it was lockdown and he was paying for the man's silence as much as the short flight itself. And the ploy had worked better than he could have expected. If the boy had any doubts about the identity of the eagle, then he hadn't voiced them, and the owl's short flight had taken it mercifully close to the crows on the line, who responded as he had hoped. Which was just as well, for he had no contingency plan to shift the crows, and was loathe to upset the boy again. He had been fortunate to have seen the same rainbow the boy must have seen, and luckier still to guess that this was where the boy was heading when he set off from home. A final disappointment now could push the boy to a place where Harpreet Singh couldn't guess, or follow.

In some ways he wish he hadn't started the boy off in the first place with his bellicose talk of wars and talking creatures. Pandering to the boy's imagination had only delayed his ultimate understanding of the truth about the virus.

But it had been fun. The type of fun he hadn't had for a long while and, as he followed the owl trainer back down the passageway, watching him walk quickly back down the road to where he had left his car, Harpreet Singh thought about their time together and his preparations for the boy; making the paste for the camouflage, distributing the items around the garden for the scarecrow, pulling the pellet from the crow he had managed to shoot and then deposited beyond the hedge, cutting and then peeling the bark from the birch saplings for the catapult.

It had taken him back, to his own boyhood, carefree days in the Punjab, of running amok in the heat and dry dust of their new home in India. Fun times, but always tinged with the lingering sense of their loss at partition. His father was too proud to ever speak about it, and Harpreet was too young to appreciate their change in circumstance and the damming news that the new nation of Pakistan didn't want them. It would take another thirty-five years and a final deployment to control the riots in the country's capital to let him know that India didn't want him either. The following year, disgusted and disenchanted, he had left for England, a single man past his prime in an alien culture. But anything was better than the death he had seen on the streets of Delhi in '84.

The falconer had long gone and darkness almost taken complete control of the evening as he took a final look towards the front of his property. He could barely see the electricity line now. Further along, he saw the light go out in Mrs Proudfoot's living room and, for a moment, the old Sikh thought about his earlier actions. It was no worse than she deserved, and he recalled how she had taken what appeared a great glee in the slow decline of Rosie's illness. Later he was to learn that all her solicitous chats with Rosie had been liberally shared up and down the street with anyone who would give her the space to gossip. An angel of death, he knew her as, hovering her wings and waiting for the lights to go out. Maybe he should have carried on squeezing.

But she was not worth the effort, and instead the old man turned and walked down the side of the house, to the backdoor, into the cold, dark interior. He still saw her when he entered, but with her came warmth and light, and he would immediately smell whatever she had prepared for their dinner. She might say something, comment on the weather, or what he'd been doing. But always she would smile, an expression which held so much for both of them, both late starters in life with much to make up. After dinner they would get ready for bed, she looking up from her book, stopping to carefully unwrap his turban, letting his long, greying hair drop like a waterfall, and then sometimes she would ask him to keep still while she combed her way through it with languorous, easy strokes…

He tried not to think of it as he noisily tugged a pan from a drawer, setting it on the cooker and looking around for the can of soup which would see him through until the following day. This would fill the time he needed before finishing his plan, before making sure that the crows, wherever else they may go, never returned to that section of the electricity line again. The boy might see his Overlords in other places, but he would forever know that Major Singh's plan with the golden eagle had been a success. It was the least he could do after what he had stirred up in the boy, the trouble caused. But it had been fun…

Chapter 21

Peter didn't see the flashing blue lights of the ambulance or the commotion of the neighbours who had joined Farmer Maguire, after he had found the body on his way to the cattle market at Halfdenport. But by then it was already too late, the corpse clammy cold, and whatever spirit had lived in the man was long departed.

But these were details which would only emerge later, largely courtesy of Mrs Proudfoot who would live off this anecdote for many years to come, but who now spent much of the morning traipsing from house to house along the street, heedless of the lockdown restrictions, her narrative gradually accreting, becoming more lurid to each successive listener, ever more distant from the basic facts of the old Sikh lying tumbled and broken next to the aluminium ladder, the upset can of tar spread like some avant-garde piece across the road, black on black, with just a little of the liquid still left in the tin. The brush had been flung many yards in the fall. She could only speculate what he had been doing up there, of course.

But when she came to call on Mrs Lassiter, she found the young mother disappointingly unresponsive, especially for a woman whose child had had certain 'dealings' with the old man. But it was a minor blip in what was to become a day of triumph for Mrs Proudfoot. Not that she wasn't affected by what had happened, but he had been very rude to her the previous evening and, even before that, any civility he had struggled to maintain when Rosie was alive, had vanished with her passing. It just wasn't right for a foreigner to be living there, by himself, in her street, the street she had lived in far longer than any of these incomers. With his death, well, she didn't know who the property would now transfer to, but at least the strange man with the brown skin and peculiar ways would no longer be living near her. And that was something to be celebrated.

Chapter 22

'Come on, Peter, keep up.' It was his father, waiting at the point in the path where field became woodland, and where his mother, carrying his sister, had already entered. Ever since the walk had started, they had made sure he didn't dawdle or drop too far behind, another sign of their increased solicitousness to him in recent days. They even seemed to be trying to be nicer to each other on his behalf.

Peter looked towards his father, then to his side where a wide field, all pebbles and rough ground, rose to meet the horizon several hundred yards away. It was a perfect day for a walk, windless and every feature of the countryside lit by a high and powerful sun. The sky was the blue of dreams and stretched wide in every direction, close enough to touch, or a million miles away.

'Here, Peter,' his father said brightly, holding out a crooked stick of sapling, one end torn into a pulpy mass, 'why don't you play with this?' Peter took the stick from his father, but he didn't feel like playing. He wasn't sure what he felt like doing, but it wasn't play.

Suddenly, an explosion, loud and nearby, shook him, and sent echoes racing across the landscape. Across the field, a throng of crows rose into the air, cawing out their protest. Peter watched as they rose, then, as if by mutual decision, all fell back down, settling on another part of the field. It was as if some giant claw had picked them up and shifted them to one side, there to resume feasting on whatever delights they had managed to find again until the noisy bird scarer swept them up once more.

Peter watched the slow motion procession with curiosity rather than fear. The virus was receding now, he knew that from the news reports, and the crows were once again becoming just another of the many creatures of the earth, unattached to millions of years of history and any more recent conspiracies. Even the blackbird was silent now, he had tried speaking with it, but the creature had only looked up briefly, as if to say 'who are you?' before returning to her staccato attacks on the ground for unseen grubs. A process that had begun with his search for the rainbow was gaining momentum, and he knew that very soon he would be leaving the world of the Electric Overlords forever.

The narrow section through the forest was short and ended at a stile where his parents stood waiting for him. As he approached, Peter could see beyond, to where the path led into a grassy meadow, its wild flowers bright in the midday sun. The meadow sloped away to a shaded dale where, tucked into the folds of the land, lay a gatekeeper's cottage, grey smoke emerging narrow and straight from the chimney. The path continued along the top of the field, next to a hawthorn hedge, now in full blossom of tumbling white.

No-one had told him the truth about Mr Singh. Instead, it had been a slow, undignified discovery, starting with seeing the cold detachment of the old man's house as he rode past. Peter had raised himself from his seat, looking hopefully for any sign of the old man, not to quiz him about the Overlords, or to tell him how many crows he'd seen in the tree at the back of the house, but just to hear the strange vowels and odd stresses that came with the man's speech, feel the life of his smile. And the ambiguity of the eyes, warm and dangerous. But instead, his only return was the vision of grass which grew ever longer, sweetpea tendrils which snaked off in every direction and the nagging mystery of the large black stain on the road below the line. He tried to make sense of it by himself, but found he couldn't.

One day, and after he had seen strange, coarse looking men, moving backwards and forwards from the house, emerging with furniture and loading it into a large van, he finally asked his mother.

'Where's Mr Singh?'

'Mr Singh's gone, Peter,' she replied.

'Gone? Gone where?'

But his mother didn't know how to answer and Peter didn't know how to understand, only suspect, which was worse. And so had begun this phoney phase of distraction and false solicitousness from his parents which only succeeded in driving Peter deeper into himself. They had tried swings and slide in the village park, then his father had ridden by bike with him to Fassingham, they had even drummed up James Ancaster on Zoom, a strange, disembodied experience for two boys when all they wanted from each other was to be in the open, running wild together. This walk in the countryside, a bedrock of lockdown activity, was their latest ruse.

It was as he waited at the stile, watching his mother lumbering across with Julia hanging on a sling before her, that he heard the birds. It was faint at first, an incessant whispering, and when he tried to look beyond the stile, into the lush meadow to see where the sound was coming from, it was impossible to tell. But as he jumped into the open field, he concentrated harder, more clearly separating the chattering from the background silence, but still unable to pinpoint its source. It seemed to be coming from all around. He caught up with his father first.

'What's that, Dad?'

'What, Son?'

'The birds, can't you hear them?'

His father stopped walking and made a show of earnest attention.

'The bird song, you mean? Yes, I can hear them. I'm not sure what they are, though.'

'Oh.'

'Sparrows maybe?'

It was hesitant knowledge and both knew it, but his father was first to react, keen to do anything to bring the imaginative child out of the fog which had descended on him since the old man's death.

'Let's ask your mum. She'll know.'

And before Peter could speak again, his father had called to his wife, who turned and retraced her steps to the pair, all standing together with their backs to the hawthorn hedge, looking over the meadow, to the wooded dale below.

'Peter wants to know what that sound is.'

With them all together and quietly attentive, the sound was all around them, and with the reflecting light and warmth of the meadow Peter felt under some sort of spell. He could see his mother staring into space, listening carefully, thinking about her son and gauging her response. Finally, she spoke.

'I think they're larks, song larks, a pair of them. Look, Peter, high, up there, in the sky.'

Peter followed his mum's gaze, and there, at the edge of the blue and almost directly overhead, Peter could just make out the two creatures, fluttering closely together, almost dancing with each other. Now it was obvious where the sweet song was coming from, its echoes spreading across the meadow and far beyond. Peter maintained his focus on the pair and, as he did so, a smile began to grow, and grow, until soon his face was alive with the emotion, and he cried out.

'It's Mr Singh, it's Mr Singh, it's Mr Singh!' and the cry spread out to the distant corners of the field, startling field mice and filling the smooth concaves of buttercups where the morning dew collects, and above, it reached the two love larks who, for the briefest of moments, stopped their own song and listened to the boy.

THE END

Printed in Great Britain
by Amazon